T0115071

A Book of SHORT STORIES

Larry English

AuthorHouse™
1663 Liberty Drive
Bloomington, IN 47403
www.authorhouse.com
Phone: 1-800-839-8640

Published by AuthorHouse 2/6/2013

Library of Congress Control Number: 2013902658

ISBN: 978-1-4817-1354-2 (sc)
ISBN: 978-1-4817-1353-5 (e)

A Gold Mine Up
Near The Sky

BRUCE WAS A FULL OF life person that really did live life to the fullest, a dare devil and not afraid to take a chance when there was danger near, this and the touch of entrepreneur'ism that he had, makes for a very interesting story. Bruce and Billy were life long friends, Billy was slower than Bruce was, and Bruce looked after Billy, like he was a brother.

I grew up in the back woods of Tennessee, almost at the end of the old country road. The Lovell family lived two miles further down the road than we did; their farm was at the end of the road. In the winter time, a regular car could not travel this road, because it was slick and muddy and the ruts were deep.

My family did not have any money, we did not have a car, but we did have two mules. We hardly ever went to town, which was twelve miles away, ten of those miles was a rough dirt road, but, sometime on Saturday,

Larry English

when Mr. Lovell was going to town, he would stop and give my family a ride.

Mr. Lovell went to town almost every Saturday morning, and he would let our family ride for fifty cents, and if we rode home with him that night, it was another fifty cents. What was so good about that was he would take eggs or butter or milk as payment, and we had plenty of that.

Mr. Lovell had an army truck that was a four wheel drive, it would always go through the mud, my family rode in the back of the truck and that was more fun for us kids, than anything else that we would do all day.

Bruce always set in the front seat with his Dad and Mom, if she was there that day, sometimes she did not go to town with them. We had to stop in the edge of town and drop Bruce off so he could go to his piano lessons, Mr. Lovell went back after him at noon that day and then Bruce was with us the rest of the day. The movies did not start until later, so we all went to the movie together. Bruce had been taking piano lessons since he was six years old, and dam he could really play a piano. He also has been taking dancing lessons since he was eight years old. I guess that is why everybody around there called him a sissy, but they only called him that to his back, because they knew what would happen to them, if he heard anyone say that about him.

I never will forget the time that Bruce stole two of his father's game roosters; he had them in a burlap bag and slipped them into the back of the truck on that Saturday morning. Later in the day, after the movie started and all the people were quietly watching the movie, Bruce slipped out the back door of the theatre and got the sack full of roosters. He carried the roosters up to the balcony and released them over the heads of the patrons watching the picture. As everyone knows, game chickens fly and make a lot of noise. The people in the theatre were all screaming and scared, and that scared the chickens more and they just flew back and forth in the theatre, making their noise. The people all ran outside and the manager called the police. No one knew who did this. The local newspaper really blew it out of proportion in a funny way; it was the prank of the year, or of all times.

Bruce and I always had a great laugh about that, the two of us are the only ones that ever knew who did it, all I did was to open the back door and let Bruce slip in with the roosters.

Not only did he seem to be good at dancing and the piano but his grades in school were the best, always an A or sometimes a B, if he got a B, then on Saturday after his piano lesson he had to go home and study, he could not go to town.

Bruce was in my class in school, and we were in the twelveth grade when he fell in love with Mary, she was a pretty girl and always dressed nice. Mary would not go out with Bruce, but she dated other boys. One by one Bruce beat the crap out of all of the boys that Mary went out with. Bruce could, and would whip anybody that was in our school at that time. He gave up on dating Mary, but then none of the other boys would ask her for a date either.

One month after we graduated Bruce left home and moved to Boston to attend college, he was still in love with Mary, but she just did not like him, and he was very heartbroken. Mary is the only thing that Bruce has ever failed at, and it made him sick.

We never saw Bruce anymore for eight years. He was up in Boston in school all of that time, and then he came home to his Mother and Dad's farm, before he started his new job.

I got a job in a small hardware store after graduation, I was the only employee, and just the owner and I worked the store. After I had been there five years the owner had a heart attack and died, I ran the store for six months alone, then the owner's wife ask me if I would like to buy the store. I bought the store from her, a payment every month for five years and the store was mine. Building, stock, and business, all on six acres, and she charged me no interest, it was a good deal. I had expanded the business and was now selling a lot of sporting goods, like guns and ammo and all kinds of fishing equipment, even a few boats and motors. I ran this business by myself during the week but on Fridays and Saturdays I had a man to come in and help me. I was doing okay.

One Monday morning just after I opened the store, Bruce walked in. We set there and talked for two hours. We had gone all thorough high school together; he was the best friend that I had ever had. I found out that he still had a crush on Mary. It saddened me to have to tell him that Mary had been married two times and divorced two times and had a child by each of the husbands, but I did tell him, he picked the phone up right then and called Mary and ask her for a date and she said okay, they went someplace and stayed four days. I guess Bruce was satisfied about Mary then, because he never mentioned her again.

Bruce was in the process of changing jobs, he had been working in the state of Virginia, I do not know at what, he never would say, and I ask him two times. He was now going to Washington, D.C. to be a body guard, and he never would say who it was for, but he did tell me that it was a Government job. Bruce seemed to be full of secrets, he had always succeeded in whatever he attempted to do, and I am sure that he will do the same with this new job.

Bruce stayed with his parents for two weeks. He had no car and only drove his Dad's truck. He wanted to spend the time with his mom and Dad because he knew that they were getting old. I went to his home for visits on two different occasions, and the four of us just set on the porch and talked. On a Monday morning, I was there when a car came after Bruce. A driver in a chauffer's uniform knocked on the door and asks for "Mr. Lovell", Bruce got into the back seat and he and the driver left, Bruce's dad heard the driver tell Bruce that his flight left in three hours.

Mr. and Mrs. Lovell were in my store regularly, and they always told me where Bruce was, but even they could not tell me what he was doing because they did not know. Mr. Lovell said that Bruce had to be doing something illegal and that's why he could not talk about it.

Bruce and I graduated in nineteen forty one, I barely made it, and he had the best grades in the class, as usual. The two of us had a lot of secrets, we did a lot of things together that was not exactly nice, and some of it was bordering on being illegal, but none of it was really bad. We had a good time all thorough school. At that time we did not realize it, but now as we look back I suppose that we really had everything. When we get the chance to talk we can talk for hours about what all that we did. While in the eleventh grade we both were going to quit school and move to Alaska to look for gold, then we got a summer job helping to build chicken houses to finance our trip to Alaska, then we found out how cold it was there and we decided to go to South America instead, we never did go anyplace.

That was nineteen forty one, this is nineteen sixty five. Mr. Lovell was here in the store this morning and told me that Bruce had been presumed dead. He had gone to China on business. He was with a group of six people that were in the CIA. They were all arrested for being spies and sent to different places for some reason. Two of the group were released almost a year later and sent back to the United States, none of the others have been heard from since that time.

The Senator from Tennessee contacted the State department and got this much information. No one knows where Bruce Lovell is, or if he is still alive, but we do know that he was working under cover for the CIA.

I do not care what the reports from the Government say, Bruce will be back, this is what I believe. Bruce was smart, strong, and active and he could handle whatever comes his way.

My business got better, I was so busy all of the time that I kind of forgot about Bruce, I always had him in the back of my mind, but time was moving on. Three more years passed and it seemed as though time was just flying by.

I got a phone call late one night, it was Mr. Lovell, and I immediately thought that something was wrong with one of them, but he said they were okay. He asked me if I could come over to their house right now so I left immediately. This was highly unusual, and I knew that something was wrong.

Bruce was at home, he met me at the door. We all sat there and talked until after daylight, and then after we ate breakfast, I went home.

Bruce had whispered to me and said not to ask questions about his job or where he had been, that he would tell me all about that later, he said that these things are not ever to be told to his parents. Whatever he told me, he knew would always be just between us.

Bruce had wanted a Government job because of the retirement and other benefits that they offered. His education qualified him for just about any job that he wanted, so he applied to the civil service for a position of a body guard, and got it. From this point on his life was one big secret, he would not talk about it. But after several years Bruce is back home for a while. The rest of this story is what Bruce has told me, in his words.

The first time that I went to China was with a party of eighteen members of the CIA. Some were body guards for Harry S. Truman, some were communications experts and some were translators, Chinese and Russian. We were in Beijing, China for two weeks for a high level meeting between three countries. We, the security people, never was involved with the meat of the business at hand, we were just there to protect our Government officials.

We were all equipped with pistols; there was a squad of seven men armed with machine guns and two helicopters with Gatling guns. The men and machine guns stayed on board Air Force One, no one ever did know that Air Force One had that much fire power on board, but it did. Any Air Force plane that had the president of the United States on board became Air Force One, automatically. Secrecy was our way of life, if anyone knew our schedule; our lives were in great danger. The helicopters were always near air force one.

This was my first trip to China, but there would be several more to come. Although we were not involved with the high level meetings there were still small tidbits of information that we heard and we could put them together and sometime it would make sense. Right now it seemed like Russia and China were in cahoots with each other and was going to back North Korea in some kind of war.

My first trip here was with the president, but the next few trips were with the Secretary of State and the Secretary of the Navy. All of my crew was just grunts, guards, we were all expendable. The translators were very important and knowledgeable people they knew everything that was going on.

In Beijing, we became part of the scenery in the office of the people's headquarters, where the people's dignitaries had their offices. I could not speak Chinese but I spent so much time there that I still had a friendly way with them. A hand shake, a smile, any gesture of friendship meant a lot. Possibly, it was against the rules, but no one ever told me or my group not to associate with the Chinese people.

One Chinese lady that worked there in the office was nice and she was as friendly as she could be, to me that is, but not to everyone. I was warned by one of my group, that, that Chinese lady was after me and all she wanted was to work her way into America. I decided to let her have her way for a while, and see just what would happen. By doing my very broken Chinese few words that I could speak and hand motions, I ask her to go out with me. She said no by shaking her head no, and walking away. I did not know if it was an insult to her or not, but she never told anyone about it, and neither did I.

One month later she looked at me and smiled and said "okay". One word is all she said. She slipped out of her house and met me in a restaurant. We could not talk to each other but we both knew what we wanted. I wanted sex and she knew that. She wanted a way to go to America and did not want me to know that. The first time out we ate dinner in a nice restaurant, the second time out we spent two days in a hotel, we used room service for everything we wanted. We did not leave the room for two days and two nights. One reason was she was afraid someone that she knew would see her. I did not realize how serious this was for her. Later I found out that she would be put out of the family, dishonored and disowned by her family and friends.

Her father believed in the old Chinese law and customs. He would never allow her to marry a person from another country, and   to sleep with someone without marriage was the worst of all, punishable by death in some parts of China.

Even if her father blessed the marriage, the ceremony lasted five days and then a fortune teller had to approve the marriage and set the date, this made it all impossible, for me. Of course this is their custom and law, not mine, and I was not interested in marriage, all I wanted was a partner for sex.

In Beijing, China everyone worked and it seemed like everyone was poor. There were no fancy cars and fancy clothes, or fancy houses they just eat well, mostly rice.

Lynshu was a perfect Chinese lady with a high degree in education. At first I did not know this, but that alone indicates that she was from a wealthy family. She held a high position in the Chinese embassy that I was assigned to. Both of us could be in a lot of trouble if our arrangement was found out.

Every week we managed to spend a few hours together. We tried to teach each other two or three new words every time we was together and now we could both carry on a conversation, almost.

Lynshu was very afraid of her family discovering her secret meetings with me. She decided to request a transfer to the embassy in Moscow, Russia. I did the same thing and in five weeks my transfer was approved. I rented an apartment in Moscow, just a few blocks from the Chinese embassy. Two months later, Lynshu was transferred to Moscow and rented an apartment close to mine. It was not safe for us to live in the same apartment. Our meetings were now a lot easier; they were more often and lasted longer.

Lynshu and I had been together for almost three years by now, someone had been asking questions about her in the CIA headquarters and we both knew that, more than likely, it was her father. We tried to find out who it was, but because of the secrecy, there was no way.

We were both scared because of Lynshu's family. This is when I found out that her father was some kind of mayor in her village. He was a very successful business man, and was very wealthy. This was also about the same time that we found out that Lynshu was pregnant. Now we really do have a problem.

We had traveled from China to Russia two or three times. We had to go thorough Mongolia on those trips and it was huge mountains with wide beautiful valleys and we both liked the place. We had spent a few weekends in Ulaanbaatar, Mongolia on our time off. So, we both took some time off from our job and stayed in Mongolia.

I bought a gold mine, there in Mongolia. The man that sold it to me was honest about the deal. Up front he told me that the land belonged to the people's republic of Mongolia. It was illegal, but the two men would show me where the place was and how they mined the gold, for one thousand American dollars. I went with them to the place where they found gold. It was the most remote place that I had ever been, or that I had ever heard of. A horse or mule could not go, they neither one could climb up the rocky mountainside, so we had to carry all of our supplies in backpacks. It was a three day walk.

The first day there I found over an ounce of gold, both of the other men found more than I did. I had never done this before, and did not know how, but I learned fast. We all found some gold every day. It was there in a small stream of water. We used pans to find gold in the sand and gravel, on the edges of the stream.

I ask them why they were quitting doing this. They both said that they were rich enough and had enough money to live the rest of their lives. I ask why they sold it to me for one thousand dollars; they said that I was the only person that they knew that had that much money. Most people in Mongolia are lazy and very poor. We found this gold by accident, while hunting for goats for food. We have been here panning for gold for six years and it made us wealthy, but remember, you must be very secretive about it or you will go to prison, if you are caught.

We were there five days, I had six hundred dollars worth of gold, and they had more than I did. Both of the men were Russian and they both said that they were going to the United States of America in a few days. When we got back to Ulaanbaatar I paid them the money and I never saw them again.

Lynshu was pregnant and was showing. We were married in Russia by a minister that could not speak English, but Lynshu could understand everything he said and I could understand some of it. Anyway she could tell her father that she was married.

Lynshu went home to her family to have the baby; I went to the goldmine to make my fortune. I worked every day, all day, and I found gold every day. My problem was food, I could not carry enough to do more than two weeks, and all I drank was water. I could not have a fire because the smoke could be seen for miles. I was very illegal and I knew it, I was close to the Chinese border but I was pretty sure that I was in Mongolia; I just did not know where the line was.

I had over two pounds of pure gold and no place to sell it. I hid the gold and kept one ounce in my pocket, and then I went down into China to find a buyer. No place could I find anyone to buy gold.

Eventually I went back to the CIA headquarters and begged for my job back. I got the same job back that I did before, which was just a guard, but if any dignitaries come to the area I was assigned to them as a body guard. By working for the civil service I was free to travel in Russia, Mongolia or China. Now maybe I could sell my gold.

I went to Beijing to look for Lynshu; I had the address so I just hired a taxi to take me to her father's house. It was very hard for me to go there but it was something that I just had to do. Lynshu saw me before I got to the door and she come out to meet me. It was a very pleasant surprise when she told me that her father was okay with our marriage and that I was from another country. Lynshu was an only child and her father was thrilled with his new grandson.

Lynshu and I had a baby boy, I was thrilled also.

Then we went into the house and I met her mother, she could speak no English and she was surprised that I could speak enough Chinese to carry on a conversation. Lynshu's mother was totally taken by our son; she held the baby in her arms all of the time. I think she thought that we were going to leave and take the baby with us.

I told Lynshu about the gold. She said that she did not know anyone that may be able to buy it, but that her father may know someone. Her father would be home from the office about dark.

I was received and accepted by both of Lynshu's parents, I may not have been if it had not been for our son, I do not know.

That night after her father came home we sat there and talked about everything. We discussed my job with the CIA, and how much time that I had off, how often that we could visit with them and could the baby stay with them while we worked. I was lucky that he could speak some English.

The next day I went to work with the father. I was very impressed with the office and with his staff in the office, and the amount of business that he was doing. He was a purveyor; his company bought goods and machinery and resold them to the customer. The goods were already sold before he bought them. He could locate just about anything; I would wait and let Lynshu talk to him about the gold.

I stayed there for a week, I was treated like a son that they had always wanted but never did have. But now it was time for me to leave and go back to work.

Lynshu would talk to her father about the gold and about selling it. I would not be back for ten weeks, I had to work for sixty days at the Embassy and then go back to the gold mine for a few days, my plan was three days to walk there, two or three days to pan for gold, then three days to walk out. Then I could go back to China for a visit with Lynshu's family. Every sixty days I had two weeks off.

I worked my sixty days at the Russian embassy, and then I slipped into the mountains of Mongolia and climbed the rocky and steep mountains, and found the small stream where I found the gold before. I carried a yard rake with me this time and as soon as it got daylight I raked sand and gravel from the stream to the edge of the bank, when the sun shined on it you could see the gold, not big pieces, but a lot of tiny pieces.

Some were half as big as a pea. In two days I collected a coffee cup full. I guessed it to be eighteen to twenty ounces.

The weather is my biggest concern with this new endeavor. I can only do this in June, July and August. Weather changes fast here. That mountain is eleven thousand feet elevation, and the wind blows all of the time, in summer the temperature in the daytime is forty to fifty degrees, and that is in good weather, and at night it is twenty to thirty degrees. In September it snows, it would be impossible to get out of there with snow on the ground, even when there is no snow it is so steep and rocky that it is almost impossible to walk. Probably the reason that no one has ever found this place and the gold deposits that are so plentiful here, is that it is almost impossible to get up here.

As I was on my way from the farm to the nearest town to catch the train into Beijing, I was stopped by the Chinese police; they questioned me about what I was doing here in their country. I had my identification card from the CIA, but I was kept in jail until the next morning. When the police called my office, to see if I really was who I said I was, and then, I was released from jail and they carried me to the train station, they did not want me here in their country.

I had some gold in my pocket that I had found on this trip to the mountain. I had it divided and put into two small plastic bags, one in each front pocket of my pants. They did not search me, I was lucky.

The train only stopped one time before we got to Beijing. When we got there I got a cab to take me to find Lynshu's parents home. I had been there before, but I could not find my way around.

I had the funny feeling that someone was following me, I must be wrong; I am just jittery from spending the night in a Chinese jail. I told Lynshu about my feeling and she told me that I was probably wrong, but to be sure we will give it a test. We waited a couple of hours then she walked down the street and crossed over to the other side. She watched me when I left; she walked down the other side of the street as I walked to the market that was five blocks away. Lynshu did not speak to me in the market place, but motioned "yes" before she walked out and walked towards home. I then knew that I was being followed. I got a cab and drove around in the area before going back to the house.

I was being followed, but why? No one knew about the gold. I had broken no laws, it had to be that I was an American and I was not only in their country but I was deep into their family community. No one ever contacted me and I never did find out why I was being followed.

Gold hunting was over with until next summer. I now had to find a market for my gold. Mr. Lang,

Lynshu's father, is trying to locate someone that deals in gold. I have fifty four ounces that I have found on the mountain.

When I got back to the embassy I volunteered to be on duty straight thorough until June 1. That way I could have off the three months of summer. I had my apartment still rented, I had decided to just work all of the time, with no time off, so that I could gold hunt all next summer, and then retire. Lynshu could visit me here when she wanted to, and she did, trouble is she brought her Mother and Father with her on the first visit.

Mr. Lang had found a dealer for the gold. Two hundred dollars per ounce and that is a good price. He would take it back to Beijing and sell it, and Lynshu would put the money into her bank account.

Also Mr. Lang offered me a deal to go partners on the gold hunting. He would send a man with me to help hunt the gold; he would send a car one time each week with supplies that we needed and take the gold away and sell it. My part of the money would be there in Lynshu's bank account. I would get seventy percent and he would get thirty percent. It was a good deal for me but it was a good deal for Mr. Lang also. We both agreed on this deal.

Although I legally had no time off for this entire winter, I someway managed to get a weekend off.

Lynshu was in Beijing, and I did not have enough time to go there, so I just went to a hotel that was just across the line in Mongolia. I had three days there, on the second day someone knocked on my door; it was the Mongolian people's police. They arrested me for spying.

There happened to be a government tower of some kind on a nearby mountain, they accused me of trying to find information about it. There were two Russian police and two Mongolia police there, they arrested me and put me in a jail, there in Mongolia.

Twenty days later I was still there in jail. I could call no one for help. I offered them my identification papers and they would not even look at them. Sixty days later I was still there and now I was being sent out to work on a farm with nine other prisoners and we all had chains bolted to our legs so that we could not run.

None of these guards could speak or read English, neither could the other prisoners, some were Mongolians and some were Russians. I could only speak English and some Chinese.

After over a hundred days, Mr. Lang found me. He had enough connections with the Chinese officials that they helped to locate me and arrange for my release. Mr. and Mrs. Lang and Lynshu, with my son, came to the prison in their car and picked me up.

When I went back to my job at the embassy I had been discharged. When I told the commander what had happened, he called the police officials over in Mongolia and found out that I was telling the truth. This started an international investigation. I was a CIA member, I was captured, the United States called it kidnapped, and held prisoner for no reason.

I was told to go back home and wait until I am called. I was still being paid and I was still a CIA member, but I can't be on full duty until this is settled. Because Russia and Mongolia police are both involved, it could be quite a while. I went home with Lynshu and her parents to Beijing and just waited on that call from the Russian embassy, but two months later, I had heard nothing.

I went back to my apartment, then to the embassy and checked in. I was not on the schedule for work and they told me again to wait until I am called. It was only two weeks until time to go back to the mountain so I started getting my supplies ready to go look for gold. Mr. Lang's helper that was going with me could not go for another month, so I decided to go on and work just like I did before.

This time Mr. Lang took me as far up the old road as his car would go, then I started walking. He said that he would be back there in one week with supplies and to see how I was.

I walked all night, and when daylight came I was close enough to see the tops of the mountain, it was completely covered with snow and ice, there was no way that I could even get up there, and if I did I could not work, and at night I would freeze. I climbed up as far as I could go, before I got to the snow. I could not leave for home now, so I decided to work the stream down near the bottom and see if there was any gold down there.

I found a waterfall that was about twenty feet high, I decided to work below that waterfall until the snow melted and I could get back to where I found the gold last year. This was the same stream, but last year I was at least two miles further upstream. This water was ice cold and my rake was left up on top when I left to go home last year. I found a crooked stick to rake the gravel from the stream, and I raked a place about fifty feet long, but now the sun is down below the top of the mountain and is not shining bright down here in this deep valley. I need the bright sunlight to shine on this gravel so that I can see the gold, if there is any.

I did not go to work the next morning until the sun was high in the sky. I was warm in my sleeping bag and resting really good, But I got up anyway, and eat breakfast, because I was anxious to see what I could find in the gravel that I had already raked out of the stream.

The bright sun reached where I was about an hour before noon, and I figured that there would be three hours of bright sunlight shinning on this stream where I was, if it was not cloudy.

The sun was bright, the sky was blue, and when I got down on my knees to look at the gravel beside the stream, I could not believe what I saw. A small piece of gold, it was flat and about the size of my thumb nail. Four feet from that, there was another, and then another. In the sand and gravel that I raked out yesterday, in about three hours I had found a cup full, I guessed at the weight and it was at least twenty ounces. Then I got down on my knees again, this time to thank God for leading me here to this place.

I went through the gravel again and found several small nuggets and small pea size pieces of gold, and picked every piece up. I then raked more sand and gravel from the stream so that I could search thorough it tomorrow.

Seven days later I went down the mountain to where Mr. Lang had let me out of the car. He had supplies for me, just like he said that he would. When I told him about the gold that I had found, he was amazed.

He just could not get himself to believe what he was seeing, he thought it to be impossible, he could not believe it, he had to look at it, and feel of it, to believe it.

Then he said, "We better think about this some more, you go home with me and let's do some planning". I agreed with him and we went to Beijing.

Finally, the whole family set down to talk, and to plan just how we were going to work this out. Mr. Lang suggested that he go with me one time to look for more gold. He said that he wants to see how it comes out of the stream, and wants to see the land before we get to the stream that the gold was in. We decided to go tomorrow and stay for one night, that gives us two days to look for gold. Lynshu was to drive us there, and leave us, and then come back after us.

Mr. Lang and I unloaded our supplies that we needed, and Lynshu left.

This time we both had rakes. He raked one side of the stream and I raked the other side. Both sides produced some gold, but not as much as it did higher up on the mountain. That first day we picked up eleven ounces.

We decided that since this trip was a test, that one of us would go up the mountain a little higher and the other one would go down the stream and see who got the most gold. He went up and I went down about two hundred yards. I raked the same way that I did before and found less than an ounce of gold. Mr. Lang found thirteen ounces. Now we knew that the further down you go the less you find.

Mr. Lang was overjoyed. He said that he wanted to buy the land that was along the road in front of the stream, so that we had all of this for our own.

The flat part of the land was only about five acres, from the road back to the stream, then there was about a mile that you could walk with ease, but then it got rough, and very steep, it was crawl and pull yourself up the mountain with your arms, by holding small trees and bushes. This place was covered with snow and ice about nine months of the year.

We left that night to go home. The next day Mr. Lang had a person that sold real estate to find out if a Chinese person could buy property in Mongolia, he found out that you could if you moved to Mongolia, and was going to live there. He bought the land, there was about five acres of it, but no one surveyed it. It took about a month to complete the transaction, and it was ours. Lynshu and I had to live there, or say that we were going to live there.

Mr. Lang paid for the land, and hired people to put a fence across the front. The sides were so steep that no one could climb up and get into the property. He also started building a house. Now we have an excuse to be here, but we still must keep this gold a secret.

Sheep will live here and do well, so will yaks. Mr. Lang had three yaks and six sheep delivered here, mainly because they take care of themselves. Our fence that was in front of our property was the only fence for miles around here, all animals grazed free, there was no stock law. Our fence was to keep people out.

We spent all of our time looking for gold and we averaged finding six to ten ounces per day between the two of us. The weather gets warmer in the daytime during July and part of August, and we plan to go high on the mountain and stay two or three days each trip, the temperature still gets down to freezing at night. This mountain is eleven thousand feet high. It takes one day just to climb up there, and to look for gold for two days, and then to come back down, that is a four day trip.

Our first trip up to the high country yielded a total of 44 ounces of gold and that was about the average of each of the four trips that we made up there. Then the snow started falling and we could not go back until the next spring.

We did not have the equipment to weigh the gold before, but we do now.

After we got the gold sold and our part of the money in the bank, we had time to relax some. Lynshu and I made a trip to Moscow and we both resigned from our jobs. We had promised Mr. Lang that we would help him some in his business, just to pass the time away.

After buying the land and doing all that we did, we paid for everything together, partners, right down the middle, and had a total of fifty three thousand dollars each. After all expenses.

We could still be working down low, on the mountain, but we all need a break. I decided to take a trip alone and go to the Chinese farming country and see what I could learn about yaks. How to take care of them, and if they were good to eat, and if you could drink the milk from them.

After a very intense study about the yak, I have decided to raise sheep on the property there in Mongolia. We will not be doing this for a profit, but as a blind, just an excuse for us to be there, for our other business.

I got a cab to take me south of Beijing about twenty miles, into the farm country, and let me out, and come back after me at dark that night, so that I could talk to the farmers. This one farmer had yaks and sheep both, and a few cows. The cows looked different than our cows back home, they were more like oxen. Most of them had wooden racks placed on their backs to haul hay and other farm supplies on. I learned that cows would not make it through the winter up there in Mongolia without a warm barn to stay in, and they require upkeep, yaks and sheep do not, they take care of themselves.

I had paid the cab driver twenty dollars for the one way trip to the country. I had agreed to pay him forty dollars to come back after me at dark. He did not come back, like he promised. I was walking down that dirt road out in the country side in China, and I was not even sure that I was going in the right direction; I finally found out that I was walking in the wrong direction. The road got smaller and smaller and after another two hours of walking that road turned into a trail.

I saw a house on the side of the trail and I went to the door and knocked. A real old man answered the door and I ask for directions. I explained to him what happened, and he told me how to go toward Beijing. There was an old women and three middle aged girls there also, and neither of them ever spoke, only the man talked. He asked me if I wanted to sleep there that night, and   since I was already lost, I accepted his offer.

They had no beds in the house. Everyone slept on mats on the floor, all in the same room. There was no shame or embarrassment about undressing and getting ready to sleep. They all undressed and were naked in the covers. I slept in my clothes, and they giggled and laughed at me about something, and I think that is what it was. No one wore shoes in the house, and the toilet was about thirty yards from the house. A pan with water in it was there on a bench outside of the toilet to wash your hands with. There was no toilet paper, but there were pieces of cloth that you used and then you washed that cloth out in a separate place, and hung it on a wire, that was provided just for that.

I ate breakfast with them that morning; it was very clean and very good. I do not know what it was, but I think it was made out of rice. I offered the old man money for my night's stay and he seemed insulted. I left their home and started walking in the right direction, towards Beijing.

I had walked about one mile when a police truck came by and stopped, they ask me a lot of questions and then told me to get into the truck. I set in the middle and we rode about half an hour, no one spoke. Then we stopped and I was told to get out. I was right in front of the Lang's home. When I told the police who I knew in Beijing, Both of the policeman knew Mr. Lang.

The winter was long and cold. But when spring came, we had everything ready to go to our new place in Mongolia.

Before the snow started laying on the bottom part of the new property, last winter, Mr. Lang went there to walk up the stream, just to study it. He looked at the rocks, the small pools of water in places where the water was six inches deep or a foot deep. He turned rocks over and looked under them by taking a hand full of sand up and inspecting it. There at the small waterfall he pulled off his shoes and pants and waded out in the water to above his knees. He had a tin can and he got sand off of the bottom of the pool and inspected that. He found small flakes of gold in the sand.

Mr. Lang was burning up with Ambition, when he saw what he saw in the stream that day. He knew that we could not work there until springtime, but he wanted some of us to be there part of the time to be sure that no one else was there.

During the following week, Mr. Lang asks me if I would go to his workshop with him, and I did go. He showed me a square metal bucket with a heavy strip of metal screwed to one side of it. The strip was shaped like it would dig into the sand when you pulled it along the bottom of the pool with a rope. He ask me what I thought of it, and I had to say that I thought that it was wonderful, it was easy for me to see that it just had to work.

Lynshu's father was a brilliant man; he knew that there was gold there on that property. He had the connections to sell the gold, and no one knew where he got it, the money that we got paid was not on record anyplace.

We all knew that when the Mongolian officials found out about this, that it would be over with, they would take it over. Our plan was to keep it quiet, and to take all that we could, as fast as we could.

Our first attempt turned out bad. We had gone too early and the melting snow and ice caused the stream to be too large, it was too wide, and swift, and there was no way that we could work it, it was almost at flood stage, so we stayed there about an hour, then, as disappointed as we were, we just went back to Beijing and waited for two more long weeks.

When we got back to our farm, which was only five acres, we found that the water had gone down and the stream was the normal size. Mr. Lang and I decided to go to the same area that we had worked last year, to start our first full summer of gold hunting.

The gravel that we had raked from the stream last year was gone. The banks of the stream was water swept, it looked like a totally different place, both of us jumped to conclusions and was fearful that the strong surge of water may have washed all of the gold away.

It was not like that at all, as a matter of fact it was the opposite. The strong surge of water had either washed more gold down from upstream, or either uncovered it, because there were small pieces of gold all along the stream. We were raking sand and gravel from the stream to the edge to inspect it when the sun light reached us, like we did last year, but we did not need the sunlight to see this gold. That first day we picked up forty ounces of gold that was large enough to see without the sun shining on it. There were still flakes and very small pieces of gold in the gravel that we had raked out.

Mr. Lang suggested that we continue to pick up the large pieces and leave the gravel and sand on the banks of the stream just as it is. We will bring help to pick out the small particles.

We stayed there on the mountain for five days, and we already had one hundred and twenty ounces of gold. We were going home tonight to sell what we had, but just for curiosity we both wanted to use the square bucket in the pool below the waterfall and see what, if anything, that produced.

We tossed the bucket out as far as we could, then drug it back in with the rope. We did this two times before we looked at the contents of the bucket. It was un- believable, there were large nuggets there. Five of them, for a total weight of nine ounces. We now had one hundred and twenty nine ounces, that is over twenty five thousand dollars in this five day trip.

It is very hard for us to leave this place now, but if the officials happen to come here they will take it all, and we know that. We are leaving but will be back as soon as we sell the gold that we have.

Mr. Lang sold the gold while I gathered supplies for our return trip. There was no problem at all, the cash was there. We had thought about Lynshu and her Mother going back with us to search the sand and gravel for small particles of gold but it would not work. Lynshu was working the office, and Mrs. Lang was keeping our two sons. We were excited, but we all knew that we had to settle down and keep our heads. We had to be careful and continue to be secretive.

This next trip we stayed there on the mountain for eight days. Eating from cans and sleeping in our water proof sleeping bags. At the end of our eighth day we had one hundred and nine ounces of gold. We had not pulled any more sand from the pool beneath the waterfall, and we knew that there was gold in there.

Ever since I gave those two men a thousand dollars to show me this place, I wondered how they became rich so fast, now I know. They moved to the United States and they have what they want. If we stay here long enough maybe we will have what we want.

I can tell a difference in Mr. Lang. He is slowing down some. He does not have the spunk and energy that he had one month ago. I told him to stay at home and rest for a few weeks. Just come one time each week with supplies and take the gold to be sold, I will stay here and work this end of the business.

The very first week that I was there alone, I worked the pool of water. It was loaded with nuggets, in two days of tossing the bucket and dragging it back out, and searching the sand, I had over twenty ounces of nuggets, and the small pieces were still there in the sand. When the sun shined on it, you could see it glistening. On the eighth day I was there waiting for Mr. Lang and the supplies, and anxious to tell him about the more than one hundred total ounces of gold that we had for just eight days.

It was dark when the car came.

Lynshu was driving, and Mr. Lang was there but he looked sick. They had no supplies. They wanted me to go home with them because Mr. Lang had to go into the hospital.

The first day at home Mr. Lang insisted on selling the gold. Lynshu and I went with Mr. Lang to sell it, we met the buyer and talked to him a long time but nothing was said about where the gold came from. The buyer was a business man; he sold mostly cars and trucks.

Mr. Lang went into the hospital and five days later he died. Mrs. Lang did not want to do anything but care for our two sons. Lynshu ran the business the best that she could, but she did not have the connections that Mr. Lang had.

I built a barn on the property, it was enclosed so that I could park the truck in it and the truck could not be seen. I had several bales of hay there in the barn for the animals. I slept in the barn at night. I had a rock fire pit outside to cook on; this was much easier than sleeping and eating in the woods.

When I went to the high mountain I still slept in the sleeping bag and eat from cans. Up high, the gold was not as easy to find for some reason. Three or four ounces were average for a two day hunt. I stayed down low because it was easier.

When the end of summer came, I was glad. I was tired, and was looking forward to just staying home to rest.

I became friends with Mr. Lee, the gold buyer. I had bought my truck from him and paid for it with gold. I gave him ten ounces of gold for the truck.

I had the barn built solid, it was warm and dry and was a good place for me to sleep. I had bought a tractor to use on our small farm and the entire land was covered in green grass in the summer time, and in the winter time the yaks and sheep rooted under the snow and eat the frozen grass. One or two times each week I would feed them hay, if the snow was too deep.

Mr. Lang had started building a house out on the front of the property, before he passed away, but that was just for show. I may complete the house next year if our gold hunting project is not discovered by anyone. To be able to live here in a house and just walk out in the back yard and find gold, is just too good to last very long. We have been getting gold here now for two summers and all together that amounts to almost a million dollars in American money. If it holds out this way for one more summer I will finish this house and we will move into it.

Mrs. Lang has lost all interest in her business in Beijing. Her interest is now in her two grandsons. Lynshu works every day there in that business, but is not doing well; she just does not know enough of the customers or where to purchase all of the goods, Mrs. Lang has mentioned selling the business because she knows that she has enough money to last her the rest of her life.

The beginning of the third summer is exactly like it was last year. The high water washed away all of the sand and gravel that I had raked out onto the bank of the stream. The small pools where I had raked the sand from, is full of new sand and gravel. I guess this happens every year.

I did everything the same way as I did before, but I am only finding about half as much gold now as I found last year. I may have to go all of the way to the top of the mountain to find nuggets, I have not found one nugget this year and last year there were plenty of them. I rake out the sand one day and the next day I spent on my knees looking thorough it. This year I am finding about one ounce per day, sometimes not that much.

We are probably working this stream out. As soon as the snow is gone from the top, I will climb up there and look for more. For seven days of hard panning, I have six ounces of gold. I know that is good, but it is not the way it was last year. In two more weeks I will head for the top of this mountain.

As disappointed as I was, I went to the barn to sleep. It was warm and dry and I really got a good night's sleep. The next morning as I was cooking breakfast, I thought about the pond, to-day I will drag the pond and see if it has anything.

I pulled the bucket thorough that pond five times and dumped the sand on the bank. I found nine nuggets that had a total weight of about five ounces. I only covered about twenty percent of the bottom of the pool of water, but this took most of the day, I made up my mind that I would drag the entire bottom of the pool and then go home.

Two full days I drug that bucket with the rope, then two full days on my hands and knees searching, and picking up all sizes of nuggets and flakes, I got everything that I saw. A total of thirty four ounces. I had more time but I was just ready to go home.

After the drive to Beijing the next morning, I sent Lynshu and her mother to cash in the gold. They come home with eighty two hundred dollars for the weeks work.

We had already had three years of this kind of luck and then we had two more years after that, I am tired, I need a vacation. I have decided to go to the United States for a visit.

Bruce told me all of this, and I believe him because he spent money like it was going out of style. Thousands of dollars at a time, I know because he spent a lot of it with me. Some of the neighbors nearby here called Bruce "Big shot", so this became his nick name.

Bruce bought the farm next to my place. sixty acres of land and an old house. Everyone thought he was crazy, but I had seen the plan that he had drawn up, and it was a masterpiece.

Across the creek from the old house there was twenty acres of rolling hills. On the other side of the first hill, just out of sight from the road and the house, he leveled out a place just large enough for his bubble. Bruce had hired a contractor from out of state to construct a bubble, built out of clear plastic. It was heated in the winter and cooled in the summer. When snow was on the ground outside, it was seventy five degrees inside. Flowers bloomed the whole year.

Bruce did not live there in his bubble, that was a place to go to relax. He viewed nature as it was, in his own comfort. Animals of all kind were abundant there. He put food out for them all.

The old house was torn down and another new house was built, six bedrooms and six baths. When the house was complete Bruce had time to set and talk. We spent hours talking about everything, and he had stories about China and Mongolia that no one would believe, but I did believe it.

Bruce wanted me to go to China with him. He told me that he would take me to the place where he found gold, and I could keep what I found. I accepted his offer.

For years I have run this store and have had no vacation. Now I am going to close the store and take a month off.

Bruce said that we need to be there during the month of August. We boarded a plane in Atlanta and our destination was Beijing, China. One day later we were there, in the Lang home.

Bruce had a beautiful family. He was also set for life, as far as money goes, or that is the impression that I got.

Lynshu, Bruce and I were on our way to Mongolia, to visit their farm, for two days. Lynshu laughed when Bruce told her that he had promised me that I could keep the gold that I found.

We started up the mountain as soon as we ate breakfast. We never got to the high part that Bruce wanted to work, because we found two nuggets when we were half way up. We stopped there and raked for half an hour. We spent the next three hours on our knees picking up tiny pieces of gold. I had two and a half ounces, Bruce had four ounces.

I should have known better, but I admit that I found part of Bruce's stories about finding the gold false. Now I know.

We all slept in the barn that night. Bruce told me to put some food in my pocket tomorrow morning because we're going to the high top, and were not stopping until we get there.

We left at daybreak, we walked fast, and we climbed the rocky slopes until almost noon. We were not completely to the top but we were almost there. Bruce said that this was the highest point that he had been.

The stream was very small here, some places there was just a trickle of water. We started panning here; I was just twenty feet downstream, below Bruce. He found the first nugget and yelled "bingo", a few minutes later I found a nugget that was half an ounce and I yelled "bingo". We each found three nuggets up there that day.

Bruce said that it took as long to go down as it did to come up and we had to be down by dark, so we left.

Early the next morning we drove back to Beijing and the Lang home.

I had four and a half ounces of gold. Worth nine hundred dollars, Bruce had truly found a gold mine and he had a beautiful family; he was a very lucky person.

Mrs. Lang would not leave the house unless the two boys were with her. They were all that she had, she thought. She wanted to sell the business before it slid down any more than it was. She asks Bruce to help her sell it, and he did not know exactly how to go about it. Lynshu suggested that he should go to the man that bought the gold and ask him, because he was a business man.

Bruce and Mrs. Lang went to see Mr. Lee to ask how to sell the business, Mr. Lee knew about the business, so he made Mrs. Lang an offer and she accepted it. The business was sold.

I never did know that Mr. Lee had that kind of money, but he agreed to pay fifty percent down and pay the rest in payments, the total price was four hundred thousand dollars, but the payment would be in Juan, Chinese money.

No business to take care of, plenty of time on hand so now would be the time to build the house in Mongolia. We went there with the materials on a large truck, two carpenters and two helpers and started working on the house.

Our main concern was to keep the workers there on the work place and not let them wander up into the woods where the stream was. We made that clear to them on the first day there. I was there all of the time to be sure of that.

In six weeks the house was complete, it was not a big house, but it was warm and dry. It was very comfortable.

Not long after the house was complete, Lynshu suggested that we all go to America and see the house that Bruce had built. Mrs. Lang and all of the family got on a plane and flew to Atlanta, Georgia, then on to the bubble in the mountains of Tennessee. Every one of them did not want to stay in the house; they loved the bubble and did not want to leave it.

Bruce had bought a golf cart and it was in the garage at the house, the boys liked that so much that Bruce went out and bought two more golf carts to travel back and forth from the house to the bubble.

Not only did the two young boys like the bubble, and the golf carts, they loved living in Tennessee. Kang and Piano both wanted to finish their schooling here in America. They were both fully qualified, and prepared to begin college.

Although they both had finished their required amount of school there in China, three years of middle school, and three years of high school, they both wanted more education. Bruce suggested that they take one year off from school to rest, and they always did what Bruce suggested.

Mrs. Lang, Lynshu, Kang, and piano all settled down and were very content with the way they lived here in Tennessee. More than content, they were totally happy. And they were happy with the plan of going to college in America. Now they want to become Americans.

Bruce was in my store every day, sometimes he was there for hours, and we talked and talked until we just about didn't have anything to talk about. Then one day he said "I have a plan for us" come to our house to-night and I'll explain it to you.

Bruce told me that we could go to Mongolia and hunt gold for three months every year, and make more money in those three months than the store would make in three years. From what I saw, I believe that we can.

I ask Bruce if that stream wasn't just about picked out of gold, because those other two men worked the stream for a few years and you worked it for four years, how much do you think one small stream can produce?

Bruce told me that because the mountains were so high, and so steep, and they were covered with ice and snow for seven or eight months every year, that the weight, of the gold, and the water forced the gold from the mountain down into the underground streams, they washed the gold down the mountain, underground,and it was forced into the small streams, above ground. That is where we will find the gold. He said that we may have to look closer and work on the very small particles; it will take longer, because I was finding so many nuggets that I never looked for the small flakes and pieces of gold. It made perfect sense to me, and because Bruce owned the property in front of this stream, and had a house and barn there, I told him that I would go any time he said.

Mrs. Lang was going with us. She was going to sell her house and then come back with Bruce and I in late August or September. Lynshu would be in their new home here in Tennessee, with the boys.

The last week in May the three of us boarded a plane for Beijing, China. I felt like that I was becoming a world traveler, and I liked it. My life has changed so much, I had sat there in that hardware store for so many years that I had become blind to the rest of the world. I feel like I now have freedom to travel.

We were in the Lang home for three days while Bruce drove Mrs. Lang to talk to Mr. Lee about selling the house, then all three of us went in the truck to their home in Mongolia. The first day we stayed there on the property, and just rested up from the trip. On that second day we were up and gone by good daylight. We climbed up the mountain until we reached the snow and ice, then we started raking the gravel from the stream onto the bank, the same as we did before. We found very little, in four hours we each had half an ounce.

As we worked our way down the stream, Bruce changed his working system. He scooped the sand from the small ponds of water and put it into the pan that he used to separate the gold from sand and small rocks; he started finding gold that was pea size down to the size of a pin head. All day long he had found two ounces of gold, and I had one and a half.

That night, there in the comfort of his new house, we enjoyed a steak dinner, prepared by Mrs. Lang. Then we got our gold out and looked at it. Bruce said "put it all in one container, because we are fifty fifty on what we find"

We had the pleasure of having electric lights in this house, we had indoor plumbing too, and an electric cook stove and the whole house was heated with electricity, probably the only house within thirty miles of here that had this convenience. Bruce had the house set up with a diesel generator, and we had plenty of electricity. No refrigerator, or freezer, we did not need that. The nearest neighbor was eight miles away, and they had no electricity. We had never been to their house, and they had never been here, and that is good.

We were the last house on this road. This road did not even have a name; we did not have an address for our house, this road come to an end at the foot of an eleven thousand foot mountain. There were two streams, about the same size as the stream that we have been working, that came down this mountain, one on each side of our house. Mr. Lang and I had worked these two streams the year before he passed away, and found not one small particle of gold; we concluded that we are working on the only stream around here that has any gold in it, and we want it all for ourselves.

It was the first week in June. Bruce and I had all of our tools ready to start panning for gold. As we started walking towards the back of the lot, the first and only car that we had seen here, ever, drove through our gates and stopped. Two men with long beards got out and started towards the house, I automically thought that it was the Mongolian officials, and then Bruce said "we have a problem".

He recognized the two men as the two Russians that had showed him where the gold was. They had discovered the gold and panned enough to make them wealthy, and then they moved to America.

They informed us that they were back and they were going to be looking for more gold.

Before I knew what was happening, Bruce hit the fat one in the head with the rake that he had in his hands, leaving three or four deep gashes in his head and neck. The other one got back into the car, within one minute they were gone.

This would not be the end of this problem, and we knew it. A fighting war was not the answer, we wanted a legal answer.

As soon as we could get ready to go, the three of us got into the truck and went to Beijing. We knew that the one person that could and would help us was Mr. Lee; he had connections that were more valuable than money.

We told him what had happened, and that we wanted to buy the property that was above our farm, to the top of the mountain, and the property that was below our farm, all the way down to the river.

Mr. Lee fully understood what we meant. Within thirty minutes he had contacted an attorney in Mongolia and the wheels of crooked politics were in motion. It cost us fifty thousand dollars, twenty five thousand for the land above us, and twenty five thousand for the land below our original five acres, this was just about one week's production on our farm. page 77 gold in stream / page 78 nugget in spring

Mr. Lee called the three of us into his office. He informed us that he did not charge us anything for putting this deal together. The four of us, here in this room know that this is where the gold comes from. I have been buying the gold from you for two hundred dollars per ounce, and selling it for three hundred and fifty dollars an ounce, but you approved my offer of the two hundred dollars per ounce.

Now, we will change the deal. You take seventy five percent, I take twenty five percent. I will come to you and pick up the gold if you want me too. I will bring you the supplies you need. I will broker the gold and get the best price that I can, this deal was made between Mr. Lee and Bruce and Mrs. Lang. She owned Mr. Lang's part.

I was just an odd person; I owned no part of the deal. But I could not keep from thinking about how much trust there was here, I had never seen this before.

Mrs. Lang was a millionaire, so was Bruce, and I do not know about Mr. Lee but I do know that I was not. But my hardware store made me a decent living. With the extra money that I have made here, I will be in good shape financially.

We missed a week's work, but now Bruce owns this stream where the gold is.

For the very first time we do not have to slip around and work, so for the first time Bruce wants to work the stream down low, where the stream goes close to the road. He was always afraid that he would be seen by someone, now that does not make any difference.

We both were anxious to do some prospecting down low, and see what was there. Early in the morning we went all the way to the river to start. Our plan was to work our way up the stream, when we found gold, if we did, we would slow down and look closer. The stream was much larger down low, than it was up high.

Bruce found a nugget that weighed one quarter of an ounce; he said that was promising, and then Bruce found another nugget, about the same size. Then we came to a small pond caused by a tree that had fallen across the stream and had been there for years. We found seven nuggets there in the edge of the pond, but none were big.

Bruce said let's quit and go home, we need our buckets to really work this place, there may be a lot of gold to be found here.

The next day we drug all of the sand and gravel from the pond, and found eight ounces of gold, it took all day to do this. In the two days' work here we had eleven ounces of gold.

This was property that no one had ever been on. We both looked for anything that even hinted that people had been here before. Bruce had a piece of land that was totally worthless, no one wanted it. There were not even any animals here. The weather was cold and damp, and the stream was grown up with small bushes and vines entangled so that the stream could not be seen. We had to crawl on our hands and knees to work our way up this place. When we found this tree that had dammed up the stream, we cut a few bushes around it so that we could work.

We cleaned out the pond, but it was a long way on up to the house and barn, and none of it had been worked before.

That night we weighed the gold, fourteen ounces in less than three days.

Before daylight the next morning Bruce told me that he had been thinking about our situation. While we ate breakfast, he said that he felt like we needed to slow our work, wait until the sun is high before we start, and then stop before it gets late. This is hard work and I am getting tired.

We have enough money to last a long time, and if we get sick or hurt the money will not be enjoyed by us.

Mrs. Lang, for the first time ever, spoke up and said that "she agreed that we should slow down". We also agreed that we would only hunt gold three months each year.

Mrs. Lang said that nature would bring the gold down from the high mountains. The steep slopes and melting snow will do what it has been doing from the beginning of time. You can get the gold down low where it is easier and safer. Can't you see that the ponds gather the gold and hold it in the sand beneath the water? Why not place logs across the stream to dam up the water? Then just work the ponds?

During our discussion Mrs. Lang said that she thought that the gold worked its way down the stream and then out into the river, the small dams would give the nuggets a place to stop. Gold is heavier than the water or sand and would not be washed over the top of the logs.

From the river up to the house we had found a total of fifty seven ounces of gold. Some were flat pieces, some were round and some were jagged in shape. It makes sense that there are small particles there also, but we were after nuggets on this new, low land that had not been worked before.

Mrs. Lang wanted to get back to Tennessee, in the United States, to see those two boys. She made the comment that she would not leave them anymore.

Bruce is ready to go home and anxious to see Lynshu. He said that it was funny how money was so important and how a person would take a chance to get it when you are broke, but when you have a few bucks, money is just not that important. For myself, I am looking forward to going home, because I have never gone home before when I had almost a million dollars in the bank.

Snow will be falling here in three weeks, but we will all leave here next week. I know that I'll be ready to come back in ten months, when the bright sun shows back up to melt the three feet of snow that will cover the gold, and hide it for us, until we get back.

The yack and sheep have a barn full of hay to last them through the winter. The barn door will be open so they can go in and out as they please. The front gate will be open on the fence, and the animals can have the run of the place, there should be no problems.

On the third or forth hour of the fourteen hour flight, I fell into an almost deep sleep, I knew that I was almost asleep, but I felt like I was dreaming. My sub conscious mind was wandering all over the place, I thought about things that I had never thought of before.

I thought about the two Russians that took me to the place where we are now finding the gold, and let me have it for one thousand dollars. Would they ever come back, and would they be armed, and looking for a fight.

I wondered if that stream would run out of gold. We know that several million dollars' worth have already been taken from it, how much more gold could there be in that stream?

Mrs. Lang did not sell her house yet, Mr. Lang and I were partners in the gold, and Mr. Lang paid for the barn to be built, he also paid the fifty thousand dollars for the property. It could possibly be that Lynshu would inherit all of that, and that would be several million dollars.

Just then Mrs. Lang woke me up. She apologized for waking me up and said, "I knew that you were not sound asleep, you were mumbling to yourself, can we talk?" Then we sat there and talked for a while. She told me that the gold had been there in that stream forever, and if we find gold in any of the ponds above the logs that we placed across the stream, then the river is holding some gold that was washed downstream before we placed the logs there, and gold sinks to the bottom, some of it will still be there.

When we reached Atlanta, I thought about getting a cab to take us on home. Then I told Bruce and his family to set in the lobby for a few minutes and the car would be here to pick them up.

I called the Cadillac dealer that I knew was not far away, and ask for the manager. I told him to bring the biggest, nicest, car that he had there to the airport and I would buy it. I told him what color I wanted, and where we were, a salesman was there with the car in forty five minutes, and I bought it.

I had never been able to do that before. I liked that feeling, it made me feel good.

The next day when we were home, Henry was running the store and did a good job while I was gone. Everything was in order; he had made all of the expenses and made me a profit. It was like I had not been gone. I was not even missed, and that made me feel bad. But, I told Henry that he could keep on running the store, just like he had been doing, he was happy about that.

For the past few months I had been earning thousands of dollars every week, some of the time each of us would earn that in one day. Now, I am here earning just about what it takes to live on. I am thankful for that, but I am more thankful for the bigger money. This is very boring; I set here in the store and talk to Henry for a while, then I go over to Bruce's and talk to them for a while, then I have nothing to do.

Bruce tells me the same thing that he is bored and misses the life that we lived in China and Mongolia.

That life over there was not easy, and this life here in Tennessee is too easy, that is the problem.

Bruce told me today that Lynshu and the boys and Mrs. Lang will not be going back with us to China. They want to stay here. So it will be just you and me and that gold mine for this summer.

We talked about our plans on how to search the stream for gold when we get there. We both had paid attention to Mrs. Lang's suggestions about where our stream ran into the river, and we both thought that she was right. Our plan this summer was to start at the river and work our way upstream. This was a good plan.

Two weeks after we did all of that planning, Bruce got a phone call from Beijing, China. It was Mr. Lee and he wanted to visit us, he said that it was a part vacation and a part business trip; he wanted to discuss business with us.

We, Bruce and I, picked him up at the airport in Atlanta. On our way home Mr. Lee said that he wanted to buy into our gold business and he wanted to be a working partner. He did not know that everything there belong to Bruce, I owned nothing.

Neither of us told Mr. Lee anything about ownership that night, and no more business was discussed.

Mr. Lee was going to stay with Bruce and his family. He had the choice of sleeping in the bubble, or in the house, and he chose the bubble. I have never seen a person as excited and amused as he was to get to stay in the bubble. He had the golf cart to go back and forth to the house when he wanted to. Either Kang or Paio, the two boys, would stay with him and part of the time they both stayed, and they all three became close friends.

Then Mr. Lee said "can we talk business now"? In the kitchen of the house, at the kitchen table, were Lynshu and Bruce, Mrs. Lang and myself. Mr. Lee spoke first; he offered one million dollars for a thirty percent interest in the property and all gold that comes from the property. That was it. Bruce said that we needed three days to consider his offer.

Bruce went home with me. We sat there in the quiet and talked about everything concerning the gold.

Bruce said that Mr. Lee is a smart man, if he offered a million dollars; it is worth a lot more. I think that we can get three million from him.

I had no part in the ownership, and I already had made more money from that gold than I ever thought that I would have. I had nothing to lose. I told Bruce that Mr. Lee had made a good solid offer. Plus he has lots of powerful friends in high places, he can get things done. I told Bruce then that if I had a vote, it would be to accept Mr. Lees offer. The only change I would make is to give him twenty five percent instead of thirty percent interest. Besides that, you do not know if there is very much gold there or not.

One day went by and Bruce called me to come over to his house. When I sat down with Mr. Lee and Bruce, Bruce said, in an official and commanding voice, okay this is the way that it is going to be. I will own fifty one percent of the property that Mr. Lee helped to purchase, and all that is on it. Mr. Lee will own twenty five percent of the property and all that is on it and you will own twenty four percent of the property and all that is on it, and he gave the already signed papers to me. It was plain that the first five acres were not included. The agreement with Mr. Lee had already been agreed on before I got there. Bruce told me that Mrs. Lang accepted the one million dollars for her part.

Everyone was happy about this deal, especially me. Now there would be no secrets about gold, there would be all out gold mining done there in that place that had already made us rich. However, there would also be a new set of rules to go by, starting right now.

Someone had to be there at all times, winter and summer. We would share the winter time, each taking every third winter.

I was to return to Beijing, China with Mr. Lee next week. I could live in the Lang home anytime that I wanted to, but my duty was on the property in Mongolia.

The house, in Mongolia, was warm and comfortable, but the weather outside was very cold. Day time temperature was from twenty degrees to forty degrees and nights were from twenty below to zero degrees. Ice and snow covered the ground completely and the stream that we found the gold in was covered in ice. We could hear the water moving underneath the ice, but could not see it.

Mr. Lee was an ambitious, full of energy person. A real business man that was anxious to get started and he was the nicest person that you would ever want to meet.

He, Mr. Lee, told me that he wanted to make his million dollars back in one year. I told him that was just fine with me, when you make money, I make money.

We have not had any visitors since we have been here. We have not seen anyone on the road either; it looks like we are just living out here on the outer side of no place.

One day the temperature got up to thirty degrees and Mr. Lee asks me if I was interested in doing a test, and I answered "yes". We got the bucket with the rope and went down to where the stream entered the river. It was covered with ice out about four feet; we broke the ice up and found out that the water was only two feet deep. Further out it got a lot deeper, but we were not interested in that. Mr. Lee tossed the bucket out only four or five feet and drug it back in. He found a trace of gold in small granular pieces. We filled the bucket up with sand and carried it to the house, there in the barn we used a mining pan and found that it was saturated with gold. That one bucket produced one fourth of an ounce.

Mr. Lee got up early the next morning and told me to come on, were' going to Beijing. He bought a four wheel drive cart with snow tires on it, an electric heater for the barn and six five gallon buckets. We could carry sand to the barn and pan it there in the warm.

A large rock was just above where our stream entered the river, so the river was not swift where we were working. We had both been bored, but now we have something to do. The first day that we were going to work on this, with the new cart it snowed so hard we could not see, so we had to wait three days until it quit, then the snow was three feet deep and we could not work. We both decided that when we got a good day we would just haul dirt from the river, and pan it on bad weather days.

Again, Mr. Lee said, come let's go back to Beijing, I have bought the wrong tool to work with. We need a snowmobile. So we went back to Beijing and he bought a snowmobile, three pistols, and three hand phones. He said that we must be prepared.

Soon we will have many thousands of dollars here and this country is full of poor people and thieves, when they find out about this, they will come.

Beijing is a ten hour drive from here, but driving there is better than the boredom of setting in the house with nothing to do.

While in Beijing I stayed in the Lee home with him and his wife. I have never seen a house as big and as nice as their home was, it was gated with a person on the gate at all times. Mr. Lee bought the Lang business, pus he sells cars and trucks. I ask him why he wanted to be away from this, and work with us. He said that he had never owned a gold mine before.

We stayed there in Beijing for five days, and when we got back to our little five acre farm, it was perfect weather. The sky was a bright blue with no clouds, it was eighteen degrees and there was about two feet of snow frozen on the ground. We now had a snowmobile and a four wheel cart and we still could not work.

We waited on that better day, and when it got there we loaded two empty buckets and the two of us onto the snowmobile and went to the river. In an ice cold hour we had the two buckets full of sand and gravel from the rivers bottom. I drove back home, and my hands were so cold that they were numb, I could not even feel the handle bars on the snowmobile.

When we warmed up we went to the barn to pan the sand that we had. It was extremely exciting when we found two nuggets in the first pan full. In the two buckets we had about four ounces of gold, some of it was nuggets and some was particles, a lot of it was like sand, but it was still gold. In a joking way, Mr. Lee offered to sell me his part of the business for ten million dollars.

The next day we did no panning, we just hauled sand to the barn until every bucket was full. It took us a week to pan the sand that we had, and the river gave us fourty five ounces of gold.

Mr. Lee's idea was to pan gold until we had ten containers full of gold. Then take it to his buyer. One small plastic container held ten ounces.

It was only three weeks until Bruce would be back. It would be a good thing if we could tell him that we had panned one hundred ounces of gold from the river, during the winter. So, this became our goal. We both worked hard to make this happen, and two days before Bruce was to get back, Mr. Lee and I filled the last of the ten plastic bottles with gold.

We had the gold in the truck with us when we picked up Bruce from the airport. He could not believe it when we told him that we had both been working almost every day and some nights, panning there in the barn. He thought that we were joking, but when he saw that ten plastic bottles full of gold, he believed it.

Twenty miles from Mr. Lee's home, and on the waterfront, was an old friend of his. We stopped there and went into Mr. Lee's friend's beautiful home. His wife and five kids were all introduced to us, and after drinking a cup of tea, we all four went to an outer building that was his office.

Mr. Lee's friend sold construction equipment, and he was the buyer of the gold. Then and there we discussed business in the way that Chinese people do business. We agreed on the price per ounce for the gold that we found. We were told up front that it was a discounted price, but it was a good price. We were happy with it. No reports would be made to the officials, because if they knew about it, they would take at least half, maybe more.

Bruce and I were satisfied to do the gold business in a small way, with the bucket and a rope, the same as we had been doing all the time. But Mr. Lee wanted to buy a generator and an electric sand pump. We can pump that sand from the bottom of the river and haul it to the barn and pan it at any time, is what he said.

We had just sold twenty five thousand dollars worth of gold that we never thought that we would have. Bruce and I both went along with Mr. Lee, because it was his idea to get that sand from the river in the first place. We bought that equipment that he wanted, and fifty, five gallon buckets, and took it all back to the farm with us.

The summer mining season would not even start for another few weeks, but I was already tired. Mr. Lee was at least twenty years older than I was, but he was a ball of fire, he was ambitious and very, smart. In my mind I had decided to just let him go, let him do his thing and make all the money that he could, because when he made a dollar, I made one also.

Back at the farm, we set the generator and sand pump up on the first day. We also filled all of the buckets, fifty of them, and hauled them to the barn. It only takes about one minute to fill a bucket with this new pump. Then we moved the generator and pump back to the barn. It was amazing how well it worked.

Bruce and I went into the house to eat, Mr. Lee would not go with us, and he said that he wanted to see what we had in the buckets. As I was getting my second cup of coffee, Mr. Lee came running thorough the kitchen door yelling for us to look at what he had found. Five large nuggets, from the first bucket of sand, there was probably over an ounce in all.

It was snowing hard now; you could hardly see the barn, so Bruce cooked Mr. Lee some eggs and toast and he was still so excited that he could hardly eat.

We worked the rest of the day and into the night panning the sand from the buckets there in the barn. We were not even half way through the buckets, but Bruce said why didn't we weigh up the gold and see what we have so far. We did, and we had seventy seven ounces of gold out of twenty four buckets of sand. This is the most that we had ever found in such a short time, and it was mostly nuggets but there was some fine gold that was the size of a large grain of sand.

We all three guessed that the stream that held that gold for so long, had been dumping it into the river for a few thousand years, or longer.

After resting overnight and a good breakfast we all three felt good. We were ready to finish the full buckets of sand that we had, it was snowing hard, but the barn was warm and dry and a comfortable place to work.

When we finished all the buckets of sand we had another sixty four ounces of gold and that made a total of one hundred and forty one ounces from fifty buckets of sand.

Bruce had only been back one week, and the three of us had already panned up over fifty thousand dollars worth. I was tired and wanted to rest for a few days.

We were out of sand in the barn, and the weather was too bad to get more, so I suggested going to Beijing for a short vacation, and we can sell our gold while were there.

Over sixty five thousand dollars worth since we were here two weeks ago. My part was twenty three thousand dollars for just two weeks work, and theirs was more.

We had all agreed that as soon as we sell gold, we each get our part right away.

Bruce and I went to the Lang home, and Mr. Lee went home to his family, we were going to take a five day break before going back to the barn. We set around the house for two days, thinking about that gold laying up there in that river. We were talking about calling Mr. Lee to see if he wanted to cut our rest time short, when the phone rang. It was Mr. Lee, he said "if you want to go back early just call me an hour before time to leave". We left within the hour.

We did take fifty more buckets with us. We also took enough food to do for one month.

A rock was sticking up in the river, just twenty feet out in the river, from where we were getting the sand. We used that rock as a gage to go by. We took sand from the length of the rock, and straight from the bank of the river to that rock and no place else. This way we knew where the sand was coming from.

The first day back there at the farm, the three of us filled all 100 buckets and hauled them to the barn. It took us all day and we did not get to pan any gold that day, but we knew that it was there for us, the next day.

We got up early the next morning and were getting ready for a full day of work. There was no snow falling, but three feet was on the ground. There was a knock on the door, and that was startling, because it was the first time that it had ever happened.

My Russian friends were back. We could keep them from looking for gold here on this property, but they may be able to cause us some trouble in some way, we are not sure. Mr. Lee answered the door, and invited them in. They lost no time in telling us what they wanted.

They informed all three of us that when the snow melted, that they would be on this stream to look for some gold. "Not very much", they said, but "just enough to get us back to America and to get a fresh start".

Mr. Lee acted like everything was okay, and offered to cook them something to eat. After they had eaten their breakfast, Mr. Lee and both of the Russians got into their truck and left, they were gone all of that day and all night and about noon the next day, Mr. Lee come back and he was driving a different four wheel drive truck. He went straight to bed and slept all day.

He let it be known that the Russians were gone and he never wanted that subject brought up again, and neither Bruce nor I ever mentioned that again.

Now the summer season had started, and we were all working our butts off, we were being rushed. Mr. Lee acted as though we had to get it all today, because there may not be a tomorrow. After the long hard day's work was ended, He wanted to pan the sand and gravel from the river at night, and it really was producing more gold than the sand and gravel from the stream.

Bruce was the boss. He owned more percentage of this adventure than anyone else did. He said that we were going to work on the river sand first, when we complete that, we'll start on the stream.

Mr. Lee said "no", we will work the stream in the daytime and the river at night.

It's hard to argue with Mr. Lee because after all, he is making more money with his suggestions than anyone has made before.

I do not know how much Bruce has made here, but I have more than two million dollars now, and that is enough for me to live my life on.

I got Bruce off to one side and told him that I was unhappy with the way that Mr. Lee was doing, and I thought that I would quit and go home. Bruce said to wait just a few more days, I may go with you.

That night Bruce told Mr. Lee that if he wanted to own all of the land and buildings here that he could have them. Two and a half million dollars dollars. We are getting out of this river over one hundred thousand dollars in gold every week. You can own it and run it the way that you want too. Otherwise we will run this operation the way that I say.

Mr. Lee got up and never said one word, he just left. The next night, Bruce told me that if he had accepted my offer that it would be half a million for your part and two million for my part and we will go home. We have enough money.

Bruce and I were pulling the bucket thorough the ponds that we had made last year. We were getting gold but not many nuggets. Today we had found eight ounces of gold and we were looking at it when Mr. Lee walked up. He said "I accept your offer".

My attorneys will have the papers drawn up tomorrow, and the down payment is ready. Today's find will be divided in our normal way. We will sell the gold that we have in the morning, and then go to the attorney's office. My half million was paid in full, and Bruce's part was one million now and one million in one year.

We had one hundred and nine ounces of gold to sell, my part was sixty eight thousand dollars, and I am fully ready to go home.

The deal went thorough. Everyone got their money and Bruce and I are leaving tomorrow morning.

When we landed in Atlanta we were as happy as anyone has ever been. We got a cab to take us all the way home, to Tennessee, I just sat there in the back seat and rested and thought about how much money I had. The cab fare was one hundred and sixty dollars, and I gave the driver two hundred dollars and said to keep the change. I had never felt like this before.

The next day Bruce came over to my house, he was grinning from ear to ear. He said "how about that deal that we made?" I have had time to think about it now and I am sure that we got our money out of that place. Although I'll bet that there is another ten million dollars worth of gold there for easy mining.

The reason for his trip to my house, which was one half mile, was to tell me about the cook out that was to be over at the bubble on this next Sunday. It will be steak or ribs, whichever you want, and as many as you want to eat. We set there and talked for an hour and then he went home.

This was an open cook out, any one could come and Bruce had it announced on the radio. Hundreds of people came, there had been a lot of talk about the bubble and everyone wanted to see it. The very first person that showed up was Mary. She was dressed really nice, and she was as pretty as she has ever been. Bruce talked to her for about two minutes, then he went after Lynshu and together they walked around and talked to everybody there, including Mary. Bruce introduced Lynshu as his wife to everybody that was at the party. In just a little while Mary left, so we knew what she was after.

Monday morning I was there working in the hardware store with Henry, the manager. I was never so bored in my life, but I kept on working and hoping that something would happen to change things. It was day after day of nothing.

Bruce called and asks me to come over for coffee, and I walked to their house, just to get the exercise. While we were drinking our coffee Bruce told me that he and Lynshu and Mrs. Lang were going to Beijing to sell the house, and for her to say goodbye to some old friends, and he ask if I wanted to go. I immediately said "yes". Bruce told me that Mrs. Lang was buying the tickets and paying all of the expenses for the trip. I told Mrs. Lang that that was not necessary, but she insisted. I told her that I would get a cab to take us to Atlanta and she said okay. I called the driver that brought us home before and set it up with him.

On the day that we left, I could not wait to get started. I told Henry to run the store and take care of things, because I know that he can.

When we left Beijing before, I took some money from the bank, this trip I will transfer the balance here to my bank at home. If I had not come to China with Bruce when he ask me to, I would not have this money.

We are here in Beijing for a month, I will have plenty of time to visit the markets and shops and just look around, but Bruce will be busy looking for a buyer for Mrs. Lang's house.

I have never seen Bruce as exited and upset as he was when he returned today. He ran into the house and started yelling for me, he said "have you heard about Mr. Lee?" He had a stroke, he is bed ridden, and cannot speak one word. We talked to his wife and she must not know about Mr. Lee's investment in the gold mine, because she did not mention it.

Bruce and I talked about this for a while; it is possible that it has something to do with the two Russians. Mr. Lee may have paid them off, if they would just leave, or he may have bought them out for whatever part that they thought they owned. He may have killed them; we do not know what he did.

Let's just take it easy and see what happens, in a few days things may change for the good.

We waited a few days and then Mrs. Lang said that we should go to the farm and see if there had been any activities there, any changes that we should know about before we talk to Mrs. Lee.

We were prepared to stay up there on the farm for two or three days if it was necessary, we took our food and water with us.

The sheep were all there, and so were the yaks, the barn door was partially open, everything looked just like it did before we left. Except all of the buckets were there in the barn and were full of sand from the river. We went to the house and it was just like we had left it, we looked in every room and nothing was changed and nothing was gone, the front or back door was not even locked.

We know that we are trespassing. We know that we are wrong for being here without permission, but there is a question about the two Russians that disappeared. And there is a question about Mr. Lee's actions on that last day that we saw him, not to mention that he still owes one million dollars on this place. So all in all we may have some right to be here.

We closed the house back up but did not lock it; we left it just the way that we found it, and then we went to the barn.

It was cold and it was raining, if you get wet in this kind of weather it is hard to ever get warm. We turned the heat on in the barn and it soon was comfortable, we ran the sheep out of the barn and closed the doors, we were just killing time and waiting for it to stop raining.

The sand that was in the buckets looked different, it was finer and had no gravel in it, for some reason we thought that it must have come from deeper down in the river bottom.

Sifting through the sand with our fingers, Bruce said "look at the fine gold that there is in this sand, it's loaded with it." We got the pans and started panning the sand, there was more gold there in that sand than there had been in the small stream that we worked in before.

Mr. Lee had filled all one hundred buckets full of sand. Then for some unknown reason he had left. And it looks like he left in a hurry, without even locking the doors on the house or closing the barn door.

This sand comes from different areas of the river. We panned one bucket of sand and found one nugget that was at least a quarter of an ounce, and small pieces of gold that was the size of a grain of sand. The total weight of gold from that bucket was over an ounce.

Three days later, we finished the last of the sand. One hundred buckets produced one hundred and seven ounces of pure gold.

Now we needed to go and talk to Mr. Lee, if he was able to talk now, if not we would talk to his wife. Actually this was his gold, about twenty seven thousand dollars' worth. We will give the gold to him, or give him credit for it on the balance on the loan, whatever he wants.

We went back into the house to sleep that night, then early the next morning we left to go back to Beijing, the ten or twelve hour trip seems to get harder every time that we make it, so it was the next morning before we told Lynshu and her mother what all had taken place.

All of this was surprising to say the least; it was unbelievable that such a thing could happen. Not only does Bruce have a chance in losing one million dollars, but we both may be a suspect in the two missing Russians. The less talking we do now, the better off we will be. We all four know the full story and we all four know what not to say.

We went to visit the Lee's at their home, because we are friends, and he is sick. It has been eight days since our last visit to them, and if his health has improved we will tell him about us going to the farm and panning the one hundred buckets of sand, then we will give the gold to him that we found.

But, when we got to the Lee home, we were told that he had passed away, just a few hours ago. We were all four invited into the house. No one else was there, we talked to Mrs. Lee, just trying to console her, and offering help if there was anything that we could do.

She told us that Mr. Lee had made some foolish mistakes in the past year, but she still had plenty of money to live on, and she was going to move to another town. She also told us that we were their only friends, because Mr. Lee had other girls that he slept with, and the friends that we did have, all turned away from us, because of him. We all four went to the funeral, and there was only about ten people there, counting us.

We were more puzzled now than ever. We did not know what to do. Mrs. Lang suggested waiting a few days then we will go talk to Mrs. Lee.

A few days turned into two weeks, mainly because we dreaded seeing Mrs. Lee, because of the dealings that we had with Mr. Lee. Mrs. Lee knew that we had some business dealing with her husband, but she did not know what it was. Lynshu and her mother explained to Mrs. Lee about the farm, and that Mr. Lee still owed Bruce the one million dollars on it.

Mrs. Lee jumped to conclusions, she began crying and told Bruce that he would just have to take the farm back, after getting her quiet and settled down, Bruce told her that was not a problem; we can do that if you want to. Tomorrow we will discuss it, but for now you get some rest.

The next day when we got there to the Lee home, she asks us if we would go to her husband's office next door and see if we could find any papers on our deal about the farm. Bruce and I went over there and searched the outer garage, and a large desk, but we found nothing.

There was another room attached to that building so we decided to search that also. There they both were, dead and wrapped in some kind of cloth, my two Russian friends. Mr. Lee had taken them both home with him, and then shot them both in the head.

We did not know what to do, but we had to do something. This is none of our business, and we are not involved in it now, but if we do not report it to the officials, then we are involved. Bruce told me to go next door and get Mrs. Lee and Lynshu and her mother. I hurried over there and ask them to come with me. When they saw the two dead men, Mrs. Lee said "those men were in my house with my husband just a few days ago". She went to the phone and called the police, and they were there in five minutes.

Bruce and I, or Lynshu and her mother were not asked any questions. Mrs. Lee told the police about the men being there before, and they left the house with her husband, she never saw them again.

Mrs. Lee told the three of us, in strict confidence, that my husband was always a crook, he was a smart man, and he made a lot of money, but he would do anything, and if you had any papers on your deal, I will find them and you can have your farm back.

Our biggest worry out there on the farm had been the two Russians, when would they return, and what were they going to do next? They knew all about the gold and how easy it was to pan, now that worry is gone.

Bruce suggested that we go back to the old time way of working the gold. Let's take it easy, work three months a year and stay in Tennessee the rest of the time. Also let's work the river completely out before we work in the stream. That gold in the river washed right down the stream and is setting there waiting for us to take it.

We are fifty fifty from now on. We can work slow and take our time.

Lynshu and her mother ask if they could have the one hundred and seven ounces of gold that we have now. We want to start a small business, a family business. While you are working at the farm we will have something to do. Of course we said "yes".

Mrs. Lang asks us if we had forgotten that Mr. Lee was the person that sold the gold for us. Lynshu and I will try to find a place to sell your gold for you.

Mrs. Lang went to a friend of hers that was a jewelry designer. She had the designer person to make a heart shaped pendent with a gold chain. The pendent was one quarter ounce and the chain was coated with gold. She also wanted one that was a one half ounce pendent with the same kind of chain. The designer could also sell our gold in any amount. Mrs. Lang had six of each of the pendants made up for a trail sales promotion. She did this all in one day.

Bruce and I went to the farm to start working; we bought another one hundred buckets and took them with us. It appears that this bucket system is the best way to work the river sand; it also is the way that we will be working the ponds that are now in the stream.

We worked the whole day pulling sand from the river and filling the buckets, at days end we had all two hundred buckets full and in the barn. We were both tired, too tired to keep working, but curiosity got the best of us and we decided to pan just one bucket to see if there was any gold in it. After two hours we finished one bucket. Not even one tiny particle of gold did we find.

Tired, disgusted, and hungry we quit work and went to the house to eat. There was nothing there to eat. Mr. Lee had finished off all of the can goods, we had no refrigerator or freezer and we had forgotten to bring groceries and we were both very hungry. The nearest village was about twenty five miles away, so we left in a hurry. We found a place to eat and a place to sleep. Most of the next day we spent buying groceries, and a refrigerator, and finding an oil company to deliver diesel to our place, because our fuel tank was getting low. This was all completed, but it was late afternoon and time for us to get back to the farm.

We have figured out now, that all of the sand from the river does not hold particles of gold, just the sand and gravel that washed down from our stream.

We removed that sand from the river, for the second time, and all two hundred buckets are full of that sand and gravel, and the water in that spot where we removed it is five feet deep. We have panned some of that sand and it does have gold in it. We are going to keep the full buckets of sand in the barn, and work them on a rainy day, but for now, we will work the stream.

We had two weeks of good weather, and we had some gold to take to Beijing for Lynshu and her mother to sell. We stayed there for a couple of days to take a break, because we may have only one more trip to the farm before it turns cold. Up there in the Mongolia

Mountains it can be summer time one day and freezing the next.

Mrs. Lang had sold three of her pendants already. Their plan was to sell them thorough jewelry stores. They made a good profit on the ones that they had sold, and they were both excited about their new adventure. They wanted to make some up and take them back to Tennessee to sell there. The quarter ounce pendants sold for nine hundred dollars, and the half ounce pendant sold for seventeen hundred and fifty dollars. The designer set the price on the pendants.

Lynshu has already bought the equipment to melt down the gold that we find and form it into twelve ounce bars. The person that she has found will buy all of the gold that we have and will pay three hundred and twenty five dollars per ounce, thirty nine hundred dollars for each twelve ounce bar. That is better than selling hardware in Tennessee.

Why are Bruce and I both, so money hungry? Bruce and I are both rich now, Bruce has much more than I do, but because of Bruce I am wealthy. Things have just turned out that way for us and it seems to be getting better all of the time. I had it in my mind to quit and stay at home, but there is just too much money involved here to do that.

A long time ago when I was poor, I lived on nothing, and then I bought the hardware store and sometimes it was better and sometimes I was just broke. I prayed every day and ask God to help me be successful and get that store paid for, and he did. Then later on I prayed and ask God to show me the way to be rich, and he has. All of this money that I have is not mine, ten percent of it belongs to him.

The next morning it looked like snow, and I suggested to Bruce that we pull the bucket thorough the ponds and pile the sand in the barn, on the floor, all of the buckets that we have are full already. If it snows it will be the end of work for this summer.

We had three days before the snow came, and we had a truck load of sand and gravel, there in the barn, to be panned. We had a warm house to live in, plenty of food and a thousand gallon tank full of diesel, for the generator.

Slowly we panned all of that sand and some buckets had a little bit of gold and some had a lot, we got eighty more ounces from the sand from inside the barn. We were both satisfied and we were both ready to go home, the equipment is already in the barn out of the snow, so tomorrow we leave here for Beijing, and then Atlanta.

I thought that everyone would be ready to go to the airport and then on to America, but we can't go for another week. Mrs. Lang has sold her house and can't leave for a few more days.

Mrs. Lee found her a buyer that said that she had the cash, and Mrs. Lee is here at the Lang's home helping to put the deal together. But when the time came to close on the house deal, that lady did not have the money, so the deal fell through.

Mrs. Lee is alone, and being around all of us seemed to keep her going and has taken her mind off of the death of her husband. She is not very old, just four years older than I am.

With that business all taken care of, it is time now, finally, for us to leave and go home to the United States. A big surprise was that Mrs. Lang has asked Mrs. Lee to go to America with us, and she accepted the invitation.

Mrs. Lee and I sat together, and all three of the others were across the aisle from us. It was not long until Mrs. Lee went to sleep and leaned over on me, with her head on my shoulder and that was okay. Then she got my hand and was holding my hand tight, and then she pulled my hand over and put it on her breast. I set still for a few minutes, and then I moved my hand and got up and moved to a vacant seat that was behind us.

I never did tell Bruce or any of his family about that, and later on I found out that I should have told them.

Bruce and Lynshu had two sons that were in college. After a few weeks at home, the boys went back to school and Mrs. Lee went with them, and lived with them for a month, she said that it was a change and she wanted to see a different part of the country.

After Mrs. Lee got back home to Bruce and Lynshu's house, I told Bruce about the incident on the plane, he just said "I do not know for sure, but I'll bet that she got what she wanted from those young boys and maybe some of their friends too." Nothing else was ever said about it, but a week later we took her to Atlanta to board a plane for China.

I gave Henry a raise for keeping the store for me while I was in China. I also gave him a commission of two percent of the profit payable in December of every year.

Kang and Paio come home for a break and their dad ask them about Mrs. Lee. They told him that she was a wild women, and she was starved for sex, and they were both glad when she left. But, we thought that you knew that, because before we went to school that time, didn't you notice all of those trips that we made on the carts going back and forth to the bubble? She hit on us the second day that she was here.

Bruce told me that when we go back to the farm to work, that he wanted to buy a small backhoe, a tractor to pull the sand from the river and to build more ponds up our stream, we'll build a pond every fifty feet and go up as high as we can. Remember, at first we only looked for gold up high, because we thought that there was no gold down low. Mr. Lang is the one that found the gold down low. As a matter of fact we have not been up high where we found nuggets most of the time, in two years.

It is a hard miserable way to hunt gold up high like that, but My first two summers were spent up there in the ice and snow and raking the sand and gravel out of the stream, then waiting for the sun to shine on it, so that I could see the gold. That is how this business got started, and then soon after you started helping me, we began working down low, and it is much easier.

Bruce had a list of equipment that he wanted to buy, and we think that we know where to buy it. Mr. Lee's old business that he had before he died, if it is still open. He wants that backhoe, and a small four wheel drive cart and about 2 or 3 hundred more buckets.

Bruce also told me that our gold mining days were coming to an end. We have one more year to work in Mongolia, then the property and the business is going to be sold.

I am going to hire two workers to work with us in Mongolia. One helper for you, and one helper for me. We are going to get every ounce of gold out of that place that we can, and we will be working fifty fifty. The following year I am going to sell out and you will receive ten percent of the selling price. After that you and I will be retired.

You already know that an ounce of gold can be hidden on your body, and most workers would try to boost their wages by taking an ounce a day, so you watch one and I'll watch one. With two more workers we should be able to increase production at least seventy five percent.

This is the first time that I have ever seen Bruce pushy, or this aggressive. He has always been a person to plan things out the way he wants them to be, and then work hard to make it happen, and I believe that he will do that this time also. He told me that he wants two million dollars in gold, from this farm, this coming year. That will make it easier to sell the farm, next year.

Bruce also said that we are going to be there a month earlier this year to be sure that everything is set up, and ready to start work when the snow is gone from the lower part of the stream. This stream, from the spring that is on top of the mountain, down to the river is over five miles long.

In the first week of May, we were there ready for work. Bruce hired a carpenter crew to put an addition onto the barn. He added forty feet to the length of the barn; it was now eighty feet long. He also had four separation boxes built, ten feet long and two feet wide, with one inch strips across the bottom of the box, ten on each box. When you pour sand and water mixed into the top of the box, the strips catch the gold, if there is any, before it runs out of the bottom of the box. And this really works great. We have a vacuum to suck the gold out of the box and it gets the real fine gold and the nuggets.

Mrs. Lang and Lynshu are both going to operate the boxes, Bruce and I and one of the helpers will collect the sand that will be run through the boxes and Lynshu will also melt the gold down and pour it into the twelve ounce bars, Lynshu has a special room in the barn to do that in. We ran a water pipe from the stream to each one of the separation boxes, and a continuous stream of water is running thorough them all of the time.

The buckets full of sand, are numbered, and gives the location that the sand came from, if there is no gold in that bucket of sand, then we will not get any more sand from that location.

We both thought that we had a good system all worked out for the processing of the sand from the stream, then when we used that system on that first day, we knew that it was good. We collected seventeen ounces on that first day and it was mostly very small pieces, just particles. Bruce had found a way to collect the smallest particles, the size of a grain of sand. But, when it is melted down and formed into a bar, it is all the same.

This fine gold is what we have not been getting, because we did not know how. It is my estimation that we have let fifty percent of the gold slip away from us. One reason is because of the nuggets, there were a lot of nuggets and we concentrated on them.

We can dig the sand or dirt and put it into buckets and haul it to the barn faster than it can be processed. We put both helpers in there and trained them on how to operate the boxes, but either Lynshu or Mrs. Lang operate the vacuum and collects the gold. We try not to let them know how much we get, but sooner or later they will know.

Security is very important now. Before Mr. Lang passed away he said that it would come to this. Just one bar is thirty nine hundred dollars and after we work a few days without going to Beijing to sell the gold, it would be more money than one of these helpers would make in a lifetime. That is why we carry a gun all of the time. Today we have eleven bars ready to be sold, one hundred and thirty two ounces is forty two thousand and nine hundred dollars. Some days we do three bars. Thirty six ounces = eleven thousand and nine hundred dollars. We never did try this hard before, but Bruce wants to make a showing so that he can sell out.

With what I have now, some people would not think that they were rich, but I do. I have just a little bit over two million dollars and a big year coming up. I am thankful and I am ready to quit, I hope Bruce does sell out.

One thing about the Chinese people, you cannot tell about them, you may think that they are poor, but they sure are not. They dress like they are poor, and they all dress almost the same way. The houses look just alike, and the people act the same way. And, if they earn one dollar they will save ninety cents of it. They are frugal and they are very smart.

Bad news today, Lynshu's mother passed away last night. She died in her sleep. There is no undertaker around here; no one can take care of a deceased person. We have to take her to Beijing and we have to take our processed gold with us, we also must take our two workers with us because we can't leave them here.

That makes six of us in the truck, including Lynshu's mother, we just set her up in the middle, between the two men and they held her up to keep her from falling. The men did not mind doing this because they knew that it was an emergency. When we got to Beijing we let them out of the truck, close to their house, and paid them triple what they had earned. They both were sworn to secrecy about Mrs. Lang and about where they were working and what they were doing, and they both make good money so we are not worried about them.

We then took Mrs. Lang to the funeral parlor and she was taken care of. Mrs. Lang had known that she had a heart problem, and she had already transferred everything over to Lynshu.

The gold pendants are selling real well, but there is just not enough time to take care of another business. Lynshu said that we would make more money if we just sold the pendants, and not the gold, at a wholesale price.

When we got ready to go back to the farm, both of the helpers had quit. Lynshu stayed in Beijing to take care of some business, so it was just Bruce and I back on the farm alone. Bruce could see that his plan to mine the two million dollars' worth of gold this year, and then sell out, was not going to work. He told me that we are set up for four people here operating the slush boxes, and we have no help at all. We are right back the way that we were last year.

Of the years that I have been here mining gold, there is one area that I have not been too. I do not know if the two Russians ever mined the very top of the mountain or not, they did not tell me. But, I am going to the highest point there is on this stream, right where the water comes out of the ground, next spring.

We both had our sleeping bags and all of the equipment that we would need to stay for three days. We walked from five in the morning until one thirty, and then we stopped to eat. The temperature had dropped at least ten to fifteen degrees already. The mountain got so steep that you had to look straight up to see the top, but we could now see the top, and it still had ice on it. The ground was covered with loose, flat rocks, and they were so slick that they would slip out from under your feet and cause you to fall. We were both down on our hands and knees crawling, trying to pull ourselves up by the small trees and bushes that were growing in the rocks.

The stream was a few feet down below us. We had tried to go up that stream of water but it was worse walking than this is, so we tried getting to the top this way. Looking up towards the top it looks like it flattens out some and maybe it will be easier to walk.

A waterfall was just in front of us; our plan was to start looking for gold when we get above that waterfall, to see if there is any gold here, or if this is just another wild goose chase.

It got cold fast. We are both wet and dirty, but we are up here on the top of this huge mountain, the fog settled in down below us and we cannot even see the mountain below us. It must be twenty degrees and were both in the sleeping bags to keep warm; we knew it would be this way after the sun went down. Tomorrow morning it should be warmer.

We made it fine thorough the night, and this morning it is clear and cold. We can see for a thousand miles, and it is just blue sky. The sun is up and it started warming up some, and that is ever so welcome. In a while, after the temperature got up to about forty degrees and we got something to eat, we started looking around. Nothing was above us. We were on top of the highest mountain. I believe that there was ice here that has been here since the beginning of time.

We both went to the stream; it was just a very small trickle of water with ice frozen on both edges of it. A thin sheet of ice had it covered over, but I saw that nugget even thorough the ice. As I picked it up, I heard Bruce say "hey look what I found". He had found a nugget also and it was about the same size as mine. In the next hour, the two of us picked up thirty nuggets. A dozen of them were within ten feet of this mountain top spring. Mother nature spewed these nuggets out of the spring.

Bruce and I both believe that the gold comes up out of the ground and is washed down stream, as it has been done since the beginning of time.

Bruce and I decided to slowly work our way down the small stream of water. It was about two hundred feet down to the waterfall, and before we got to the top of the waterfall we had found eight more nuggets, this place was loaded with gold. From the top of the waterfall back up to the spring, there were a lot of small granules of gold that was visible, without any digging or raking at all.

We had to be careful not to get our clothing wet, because if you did, you could freeze to death, or not to slip and fall, because a broken arm or leg up here could mean death, and how would you ever carry anyone out of this place. We had talked about this and both decided to work slow, be careful, and to watch out for each other.

Our next move was to scan this area for visible gold, and work our way down to that waterfall. We have no idea how high it is, we can just hear the roar of the falls.

Two other springs were feeding water into the stream before it went over the falls. We did not have the time to look at the other two streams and search for gold, because we had to climb down to the bottom of the falls before dark, and now we had our food and sleeping bags to carry down. Each one of us had the nuggets that we had found, carrying them in our sleeping bag, thirty eight nuggets in all. We still have to figure out a way to mine the small particles of gold that we found up here on this mountain.

We moved away from the stream to sleep, because the water mist was getting us damp. We were in the sleeping bags as soon as it got dark. We had some food for breakfast, but that is all, there would be nothing else to eat, after breakfast tomorrow morning, until we got home.

During the night there was an awful noise, that woke us both up, and although it was not raining here, it was raining up there where we were yesterday, on top of the falls. I got out of my bag and climbed part of the way back up there. I saw water being blown out of a hole in the ground; the water was going at least fifty feet high. This lasted about ten minutes and then just stopped.

No one knows that we are up here. Also, no one knows that this gold is up here. If and when we ever tell anyone about this trip, we will not tell about that water being blown up out of the ground, no one would ever believe that.

This is our third day, we have no more food, It will take us all day to walk down the mountain and get home. However, Bruce wants to just spend one hour at the foot of the water fall to see if that small pond holds any gold.

We did go there to the pond. We found gold like we had never seen before, there is more gold here than there was up on top at the spring. In two hours we both had our caps full. We had no container to put gold into. We used our caps, until they filled up, then we headed down the mountain for home. It would be at least midnight when we get there, plus we do not have a light to see to walk by. Our original plan was one day to go up, and one day to look for gold, and then one day to walk back to the house. Everything changed, it was a very profitable trip, but this is very rough country with rock cliffs, and it is hard to walk in the daytime, and impossible to walk in the dark.

We did make it home; we walked into the house just after midnight, and after we looked around and found something to eat, we both just wanted to weigh the gold. We had two hundred and thirty ounces of gold, seventy five thousand dollars worth, for three days work. But we now know where that gold is.

We both are anxious to get back up that mountain to find some more gold.

What we found up there is unbelievable. Not just the gold nuggets lying on top of the ground, but the water being blown up out of the ground the way it was.

We cannot climb that mountain again until we make a trip to Beijing. We can never leave gold in the house while we work, and we can never let anyone know that we have any gold, any place, or that we are mining gold here. Everything we are doing here is secret, and when people find out about it, it will be over with.

Regardless of how much we make here this season, I think that we should leave Mongolia, and China, and go to the United States, and stay there from now on.

End Of Part Two

I TALKED A VERY LONG time to Bruce about my thoughts. I would like to see him sell out and go home, if he can find a buyer. I begged and pleaded with him but he would not give me an answer. Then I told him that I was not going to stay here in Mongolia for another year.

We decided to go to Beijing, and discuss this problem over with Lynshu, and I was sure glad of that because I knew what she wanted.

Bruce changed his mind and agreed to sell. He said that if we could sell everything we have in China and Mongolia that we would leave here and go to Tennessee and stay forever. But, if we can't sell and get the cash, then we will have to just be here three months each year and do what we have been doing.

We located a gold mining company in Mongolia and traveled to their headquarters. We both were there and presented our presentation to the president of the company. After I heard what we said, I did not believe it myself. It was too good to be true. Also, we could not tell him where our mine was, and we had no paper work at all.

Not only did we find an enormous amount of gold, with no digging, but we had paid no taxes at all on any gold and the taxes in Mongolia for mining gold is sixty percent.

I can't say this for sure, but we may have found the most gold of any mine in Mongolia.

When we got outside of their office Bruce said, "We have hurt ourselves". That man did not believe anything that we told him about the amount of gold that we had found, and that it was mostly nuggets. If anyone told me, what we told him, I would not believe it.

Bruce and I traveled almost all night to get home, and Lynshu was waiting up for us. We told her what we had told him, and she said "you should know that no one in his right mind would believe that". You may as well forget trying to sell that place. Now you are in danger of the Mongolia people's police coming after you for taxes.

Everybody slept late the next morning, and then as we were eating breakfast, Lynshu said "let's all get ready and go to the United States, just as soon as we can get a ticket. I have a bad feeling about that president of the mining company knowing how much gold that you said that you had found, I expect trouble soon. Mongolia will tax you on what you said that you had found, if that man reports you.

We ordered our tickets that day, and prepared to leave China. Our suitcases were setting by the door and we were ready to walk out. We had two hundred and thirty ounces of gold that had not been sold and Lynshu had already called the buyer. She was going to take the gold to him in one hour.

Someone knocked on the door and Bruce answered the door. It was the president of that company that we had talked too.

I felt like running, but there was no place to run to. All we could do was try to talk our way out of whatever problem that we had.

The man said that he "did not know whether to believe us or not. But, if you told me the truth, then I would be interested." He asked to see some gold, and we showed him the two hundred and thirty ounces. He then said "now I believe you". Then he wanted to see the gold mine, and that was not going to happen, Bruce told him that there was no way he could see the mine.

I was starting to believe him now, he was Russian and he appeared to be well educated. He was doing and saying the same thing that I would have been, if I was in his place.

Those two hundred and thirty ounces of gold is the only thing that he could get us for, if he happened to be an undercover policeman. He volunteered to be blindfolded all of the time, that we were traveling, if we would just show him the mine, and he said that "if it is the way that you described it to me, I will buy it".

While we were talking, Lynshu slipped out of the house and took the gold to the buyer, and Anton, that Russian, did not even know that she was gone.

Late the next day, Anton and Bruce and I left for the farm. We purposely left late so that Anton could sleep, and would not know where he was. We knew that ten hours would be a quick trip for us to get there, and Anton had agreed to stay blindfolded. If he was asleep it would be easier on all of us.

After we arrived there Bruce removed the blindfold from Anton. There were no signs within miles of here for him to see, no one to talk to and no way for him to know where he was. The only reason that Anton knew that he was in Mongolia, is because we told him so.

Bruce and I both felt like that we were in danger. We both thought that in some way that Anton was going to cause us some harm. I had a pistol in my pocket and so did Bruce, and I think that we were both ready to use them if we had to. We kept a close eye on Anton to be sure that he did not have a weapon on him. Anton did not have any baggage of any kind, but he was a big man, probably over two hundred pounds, and all muscle. One good lick from him could knock you out, gun or not we had to be careful.

I had made up my mind that if there was any trouble at all, that I would just shoot Anton, that's what it would take to stop him.

We had a one day trip planned for tomorrow. We will leave at daybreak and start down there by the river and work our way upstream, letting Anton look at what he wanted too and anyway that he wanted too. There was a bucket with the rope on it by the river, and one by one of the ponds for him to use, if he wanted to.

Anton worked hard, he knew what he was doing, and he was finding gold. We followed and did nothing but watch. He found gold in the river and the pond and all up and down the stream, he was excited about the very fine gold that we had not even tried to pick up. He told us that the whole place was loaded with gold, but he wanted to see all of it.

It was late in the day, but we had told Anton about the nuggets that were high on the mountain. It was too late to start up there today. So we planned it for tomorrow.

Anton had picked up eleven gold nuggets and had them in his shirt pocket. When we got back to the house, and while we were eating, he took the nuggets out of his pocket and put them on the table. He said that is the most gold that I have ever seen in just a short walk, and it is on top of the ground, and in the bottom of the water.

He said that if I see nuggets on the ground, in the morning, like you said, we will make a deal. He said that "I have been mining all of my life, my father was a gold miner before me, and I have never even heard of any mine that had gold on top of the ground like you have here". We use machines to dig for gold, and that cost a lot of money.

Anton is big and strong, but he was really huffing and puffing while going up the steep slopes, a few times he just had to lie down and get his breath. We thought that he was not going to make it, but he wanted to see what was up there so much, and he had so much determination, that he finally crawled to near the top at about two o clock in the afternoon. Bruce and I both told him several times about how long it took to go back down, but no use, he was headstrong and determined to see that gold. In the two streams that run into the main stream, is where he went to look, Bruce nor I, had ever looked at those streams, Anton was the first. He found at least ten ounces there. We both told him then that we were going down the mountain, and if he wanted to stay that he could, but we were gone.

Anton stayed up there all night. No sleeping bag or anything to eat. He laid down right there by the two streams and never slept any because it was so cold. But he kept picking up gold until dark. When he got to the house the next day at noon, he had thirty one ounces of gold. He said this is like a dream; I still have a hard time believing it. We set down to talk business. Anton's offer for the place was one million dollars. Bruce told him that it was three million, but we would take two million down, and the other million in two years.

Anton said that he had the money, but it would take one month to get it. The agreement was made and the paper work would be done in Beijing when we get there.

When we got ready to leave, Anton was blindfolded again; he was lying down in the back seat of the car. He could see nothing but he could talk, and we talked most of the way home.

The gold that he found while he was there was split three ways, we all got three thousand three hundred and thirty three dollars each. Bruce told Anton that when we get the money we will take you back there and then we will leave.

Part of the deal was that we tell no one about our deal. Nothing at all. Anton said that he was going to operate the place the same way that we did, because of the taxes. Sixty percent takes all of the profit out of mining.

Our tickets to America were put on hold for about a month, but then we were all going, and I hope we do not come back.

When we went to the attorney to do the paper work, Mrs. Lee was there. She assisted with our papers being completed because she worked there. She handled the transfer of the two million dollars and the depositing of it into Bruce's bank account. When all of that was completed, she asks Bruce and Lynshu for a job. She found out that we were all going to America, and she asks if she could go with us.

Lynshu hired her as a house keeper, if she comes to America, at her own expense. Mrs. Lee had plenty of money, so she went to America with us, on the same plane.

Bruce and Lynshu paid me my part of everything that I had coming, and they were very generous. I had more money than I could ever spend in my life time. Bruce had several million dollars that I knew of, and Lynshu got all of her mothers and father's money and property. I know that they are alright financially.

I have no more money in the China bank; it is in the little hometown bank right there in Tennessee. I will probably travel some after I am home a few weeks and get tired of that hardware store.

Bruce and Lynshu went on a shopping trip for a few days. When they returned they had a book for me. The title was "how to find gold". Bruce had a copy of the same book for himself. That book said that in very cold places that the ground spews up, and gets soft, it has holes that open up and small pieces of gold drop down into the holes, because gold is heavier than the water or dirt that is around it. Every year the same thing happens, and in a thousand years or so, gravity and the weight of the snow and ice move that gold down, usually to a stream.

That may or may not be true. But it sure does sound right. Because in the place where we were we had the steep and Rocky Mountains, and we had the ice and snow for nine months of the year, and it was about four miles from the river to the top of the waterfall, then another mile to the top of the mountain. None of it was easy walking, that gold had thousands and thousands of years to sink down, until it reached our stream.

The two Russians become millionaires there on that stream. Bruce and I become millionaires on that stream, now Anton has his chance, on that stream. I know that the gold is there, Bruce and I saw it. Flakes and very small pea size gold. Anton will get that gold that we picked over, it's his, and he has paid for it.

Bruce is living the life of retirement; he spends half of his time in the bubble, and half at home or with me in the hardware store. He come in the other day with two mining pans, hid, in a bag so no one could see them. He asks me if I would go with him and check a couple of streams and see what we could find. I told him okay, it was just something to do.

After two weeks of panning, and not finding one speck of gold, we drove down into Georgia to try our luck. In Dahlonega, Georgia, where gold was found a long time ago, so we panned there for a week, and found three small flakes of gold, not enough to count.

Then on our way back home we traveled thorough a mountainous section of Georgia, we stopped near Clarksville, Georgia and rented a boat to tour Lake Burton. We just rode around the lake and when we saw a stream running into the lake, we stopped and panned that stream. In three days of that, we found a thimble full of very small pieces of gold. We decided that if we are going to pan for gold that we will just go back to Mongolia and help Anton, but I am not going to pan for gold.

When we got back home to Tennessee, we found out that Mrs. Lee had quit her job with Lynshu. She was preparing to go back to China. Mrs. Lee and Lynshu had worked out a deal for them to make and sell the gold pendants. They were going to have them made in China and sell them here in the United States.

Mrs. Lee knew Anton, and she was going to see if he would sell her the raw gold. She knew a lot of people there in Beijing, and she had plenty of money, so they had everything that they needed.

When Mrs. Lee got to her home in Beijing, she started trying to locate Anton. The only way that she could find him was to go to Mongolia where the farm was, so she bought a new pickup truck and, using the map that Lynshu had given her, started on the five hundred plus miles to Anton's farm.

On the second day she drove up to house, no one answered her knock on the door, so she went on to the barn, and no one was there either. She decided to wait in the house until Anton come in from work. She looked all thorough the house, and in the bed room she found Anton there drunk. He could not even talk to her; he could not even rise up, or turn over in the bed.

Mrs. Lee found food and coffee in the kitchen; she first made a pot of coffee, and started forcing Anton to drink it. After several cups of very strong coffee, Anton was able to walk and talk. He did not know how long that he had been drunk, or where his friend was, or where his truck was. Anton told Mrs. Lee that he had met this lady in the village and she was going to keep house for him. He thought that, that was two days ago.

Anton ate a big meal, and then asks Mrs. Lee to take him to find his truck. They rode all around the village and there was no truck. They went to the bar where he picked her up, and no one there knew her, so they both went back to Anton's house.

Mrs. Lee then ask Anton if he would sell a small amount of gold to her and Lynshu for their jewelry project, and he told her that he did not have any gold. He said that the gold had just about run out there in the stream and the only place that he could work was down low, because of the weather. He did say that when the weather improves that he would sell them what they needed.

Mrs. Lee had been around Bruce and his family long enough to know that what Anton said, was not exactly true.

Anton told Mrs. Lee that he needed to go home and he had no truck, and he ask her if she could drive him home and then bring him back? She said yes, because she had now figured out that he was not thinking straight and she wanted to find out what Anton was going to do.

Anton lived three hundred miles north of the farm in Russia, and Mrs. Lee lived five hundred miles south of the farm in China.

It was an overnight stay in a hotel for each of the trips. This is where Mrs. Lee and Anton started staying together, within six months they were talking about marriage. They talked about it for a year, but never did get married.

In Beijing, China while Anton and Mrs. Lee was there on the first trip to China together, she went to a phone and called Lynshu and told her the complete story about Anton. He drank all of the time; he was not working the gold and had lost all interest in everything. And that it may be a wise move to come here and investigate. He has three hundred buckets of sand in the barn and acts like that he does not even know it.

Five days later, Lynshu and Bruce were in China. They rented a house because they both knew that the business at hand would take some time.

Anton had to go where Mrs. Lee went, he had no vehicle and now he, as Mrs. Lee has found out, has no money. But, he knows that she is wealthy.

Anton does not yet know that Bruce and Lynshu are here in China, but Mrs. Lee does, and she has been to talk to them. They have decided to dry Anton out, make him stop drinking, and to help him get the mining deal back into operation. Mrs. Lee went after Anton and brought him to see Bruce and Lynshu. Anton was totally ashamed, and he cried.

The same friend of Anton's that took his truck, also took what gold that he had there in the house, only about six ounces. But now someone knows about gold being here, and sooner or later they will be back, and they won't hesitate to kill for it. When Bruce told Anton this, he said that he wanted to sell the farm and get out. He ask if Bruce was interested in buying it back, and Bruce said yes, but you have already taken all of the gold from it. How much do you want for it? Anton said seven hundred and fifty thousand dollars, Bruce said I'll pay you five hundred thousand dollars cash, and Anton said "okay", and they shook hands on it.

Bruce went to the farm with Mrs. Lee and Anton right then to see what kind of shape that things were in.

The barn was good, and all of the equipment that we had bought was there and in good shape and the backhoe that Anton bought was there and it was in new condition. The buckets were almost all full of sand. Anton had something to happen to him all of a sudden, and he just gave up.

I made one hell of a deal on this. I feel bad about Anton, but in his shape he would have given it away or one of his friends would have taken it from him.

Actually, he is a bum. He has done away with his family's mine that he was president of. Mrs. Lee better get rid of him as soon as she can.

One week later Bruce called me, I was in the hardware store, and Henry had taken a day off. I hated being there even when Henry was running things.

Someway, somehow I just felt like that was Bruce on the phone when it rang, as he was saying "do you want to come to China"? I said "yes", right in the middle of his sentence, but I can't leave before tomorrow. He said come on, you and I are going to run that farm again, the way that we did before.

Lynshu was very happy about all of this; she said that now Mrs. Lee and I are going to proceed with our project.

Bruce told Lynshu and Mrs. Lee that if they wanted to, that they could pick up their own gold from the stream for the pendants or you can help us with the buckets that are in the barn and we will split it with you.

Everyone was thrilled that things are working out the way that they were. But now we have to do something with Anton.

Bruce offered Anton five hundred dollars per week to work with us, and he turned it down. We knew that he had the money that he was paid for the farm when

Bruce bought it back, Anton probably will not work until that money is gone.

My first day back was spent cleaning the house. All three of us, Bruce, Lynshu and me all worked all day. Mrs. Lee was gone with Anton and we did not know when she would be back, or if she would be back at all.

We planned to work the dirt that is in the buckets tomorrow, we do not know where the sand came from, so there may not be any gold in that sand. We have about two more weeks until we can really start working the stream down low, but we can do the sand that is in the barn. These buckets of sand have the same marking on them that we put on the last buckets that we filled before we left. This sand is very dry, and seems to have been in the buckets for a long time. All of us believe that Anton did not work the buckets of sand that we left for him. Since the backhoe was as clean as it was, we think that it was never used, so we do not think that Anton worked any at all. He just started drinking and let the working season go by, then come the snow and he could not work.

If this is true, it means that no gold has been taken from the stream in a year. The hole there where the stream enters the river will be filled up again.

In the first bucket of sand that we ran there was a small amount of gold, about one third of an ounce.

The second bucket there was almost an ounce, now we are sure that this is the same sand that we had brought in and Anton did not run it. There was two hundred buckets of sand and we found sixty one ounces of gold. Lynshu and Mrs. Lee had thirty ounces of gold to start their business and that is a good start.

Our first day of work on the stream was to drag the ponds, but we used the backhoe instead of the bucket with a rope, we found gold and lots of it. The nuggets were easy to see and pick up, but there was some fine gold there, so we hauled everything to the barn and run it thorough the separation boxes. One day netted sixteen ounces, of gold.

Mrs. Lee returned late, the afternoon of that first day. She had taken Anton to his home in Russia and left him there. She agreed to work there in the barn on the seperation boxes, so there would be three people doing that and one of us getting the sand from the stream to the barn.

We have decided that we would go into Beijing every other week to sell whatever amount of gold that we have. Either Bruce or I must stay here at all times. This week Bruce is going, next week I will go. We have three pistols here now, but Bruce is buying two shotguns on this trip. The front gate is to be closed and locked at all times, and we are getting a guard dog that will stay here. Anton is the reason that we feel that we must have more security, we are not sure who he had here, or who all he told what we were doing here. Right now we are very worried about our safety.

Lynshu suggested to Bruce that, for their part of the gold, that they melt it down into twelve ounce bars and keep it for the jewelry business. After he thought about that for a few minutes he agreed, So I said that I may as well melt my part down also, but I am taking mine back to America with me.

This just creates another security problem, because there will just be more gold here on hand to worry about. I changed my mind and decided that I would keep just ten bars to carry home when I go, if there is more it will have to be sold and the money transferred to Tennessee.

Just one week later Mrs. Lee and Lynshu went to Beijing to make arrangements for pendants to be made. As a start up for the business they ordered one hundred, half ounce pendants, and one hundred quarter ounce pendants. They carried the seventy five ounces of gold with them for that, and the balance of the gold that was here, they carried to be sold.

They left very early that morning. Bruce and I had planned an overnight trip to the top of the mountain, we did not know if Anton had been back up there or not, but we were going to see how it was now. We now knew the short cuts and the best places to walk, we walked as fast as we could and we arrived at the place where we had left our sleeping bags, and they were covered and dry. We still had about an hour of daylight, so we started searching the stream for nuggets. I found nothing, but Bruce found a large one, at least one half ounce.

I can't say that nuggets were as plentiful here now as they were two years ago when we were here, but there are some. I know that the area nearest the spring was picked clean when we were here before, and now we have found more there in the same spot, I do not know where they came from.

We searched the area where the two springs dumped its water into the main stream, and found about fifty percent of the amount of nuggets that we found before. They have to have been forced up out of the ground by some kind of pressure from beneath. fifty yards from that same spot is where the water spout appeared on that night that we slept up here. There are areas between here and the foot of the mountain that we have not even looked at, and we already know that the pool at the bottom of the big waterfall has gold in it.

There is just too much area here for us to work, a poor man could get rich in this stream in two years, but the way that things have worked out, Bruce and I are already rich, and we have the stream also.

After picking up about twenty ounces of gold nuggets, we had to leave and hurry down the mountain to get home before dark. When we got home we found that we had been broken into and robbed. The house was all torn up inside, a few things were gone, all three of the pistols were gone, and the food was all taken.

There was no gold in the house because Lynshu had taken it with her to Beijing. There is nothing we can do but for us to go to Beijing also.

We have the gold that we found today to take with us. It will take us all night to drive there but we have to go, I would be afraid to stay here without the pistols but now we know to be prepared at all times.

Mr. Lang said a long time before he died, that it would be this way as soon as anyone found out that there was some gold here, and that we were mining it. He said that we would need to be armed to work here, and that the ladies could never be here alone, and now we know that he was right. Tomorrow we will buy everything that we need to protect ourselves.

In Beijing, we told Lynshu and Mrs. Lee that they may not want to go back there, after what happened. They wanted to think about it for a while.

Bruce and I tried to find the two men that worked with us before, but they were not at home, the next day we found them and they both agreed to go back with us, we offered them a very good deal to go and stay for one month, after that we will decide if we offer them another deal, for another month.

We bought guns and a dog, we bought hand held phones for the area, and plenty of food to do all of us for at least a month and then we hurried back to the farm as quick as we could.

As far as I was concerned, I was more ready to stay there and work now, than I was before. It was more interesting, more exciting, and I caught myself hoping that they would come back and try to rob us again. We had no idea who it was, but we figured that it was Anton's friend, and probably some of her other friends. Anyway, we were ready for whoever it was.

Lynshu and Mrs. Lee got back one day after we did, they had a lot of good luck with their project and were both happy about that.

The two hired men were sleeping in the barn where the hay was before, and they were happy with that, because they had plenty to eat, and knew that they would get a big payday.

The Doberman was staying inside the house until it gets friendly with all of us. We had the house all cleaned up again, and was making our plans on how to work, starting tomorrow.

A truck drove up into our lot; Mrs. Lee said that it was Anton's truck, so Bruce and I both went out the door with automatic shotguns, loaded. The lady driver comes out of the truck screaming, saying that she just wanted to see Anton.

She swore that she did not know anything about the break in; she said that she and Anton were staying together, and he would not stop drinking, so she left, but I was coming back, she said. And I did take some money, but Anton said that it was okay.

Now we have another problem. This is Anton's truck that she is driving; Anton is in Russia, what are we going to do? Mrs. Lee said that her passport was in Beijing, and she could not go into Russia. Let her drive the truck and go where she wants too, it's not our business.

Early the next morning we all went to work, the separation boxes were all set up, inside of the barn, we now had four separation boxes. One person worked the same box all of the time. If they did not find gold then they did not get paid. If they found gold they got ten percent of what they found. This was a decision that they made, they had a choice of a weekly salary, or the ten percent, and they chose the ten percent. Each person got their pay, in gold, every day.

Mrs. Lee and the two men worked every day and they all usually made two or three hundred dollars per day. They worked long hours and a lot at night, getting the gold every day was an incentive for them to work. Lynshu worked when she wanted too, but one of the boxes was hers and no one else was allowed to work it.

Bruce and I went up and down the stream and got sand where we thought it would produce the most gold. We kept strict records, written on the buckets, where the sand came from. We wanted the workers to make a lot of money, because when they made ten percent, we made ninety percent.

There is five miles of stream here, and every place we have worked, we found gold, but some places are better than others. One separation box will use a bucket of sand every hour. When all four are working that is only four buckets an hour, we can get ten times that much in one hour, but we have to haul away the gravel and sand that is left over from the buckets.

The two Chinese men are good workers, they do not talk, and they just work. They both want their wives to come here and work a box, and Bruce and I think that it is a good idea. We are going to build two more boxes soon, and their wives can live in the barn with them, and work the boxes.

Mainly, it is fine gold and small particles that we are getting now. For the years that we have been working here, we have concentrated on nuggets, but they have just about run out, we hardly ever find one down low, only when we go to the top. But it does not make much difference, because we have plenty already, we both have millions. the second month On of this season, the wives of the two Chinese men were here and moved into the barn. They all four worked all of the time, only when they slept and eat were they not working. They all knew that this was not a permanent thing, and it could end at any time, so they were making the best of it. Every night they gave us the gold that they had found that day, we weighed it and gave them each their ten percent. Each one of them kept their gold strapped to their body, and they knew that if the people's police found us, and come there to raid us, that it was up to them to save their gold, or lose it.

Every two weeks we had to go to Beijing to sell our gold and get supplies, one of the Chinese would go with us and take all of the Chinese gold with them. They may have sold it, or they may have hid it, we do not know, but we do know that these four Chinese have several thousand dollars worth of gold someplace. They are probably the richest chinese people in their neighborhood. That is what we wanted; we can depend on them to be secretive.

Bruce is pushing fifty three years old now. He always talks about retirement, but he won't retire. He can live his life out on the money that he has, and so can his children live their lives out on the money that he has. Bruce is afraid of something, and I do not know what it is because he and his mother and father have always been pretty well off. Not only that, but Lynshu has more than Bruce does.

This season only has two more weeks before it could snow. We were closing down this time last year, but this year we have stock piled as much sand in the buckets and piled sand in the barn, enough to last us at least a month, so we will go home when we run out of sand to work with.

The Chinese ladies went to Beijing with Lynshu and Mrs. Lee; the Chinese will not be back because we are so near finished. Lynshu will be back for at least a week, and then we will prepare this place to be vacant for a few months.

Before daybreak this morning, the peoples police came in thorough our gates, knocking our gates down, they were in two trucks, each truck had two policemen in it. They were all armed with shotguns, we did not know who it was at first, and we let the Doberman out, he attacked them and they killed our dog.

They searched our house for gold and did not find any. They searched the barn and there was no gold there either, and there were no people there either. The Chinese men had run and they had taken all of the gold with them.

The equipment to melt down the gold was there, but the police did not know what it was. They wondered what the sand and gravel was there for, and the separation boxes, but they were just looking for gold and there was no gold. They all four left our place unhappy, but they all left.

The Chinese men hid in the woods all day and about an hour after dark they both come to the house. We already had everything packed in the truck ready to leave, we were just waiting on them to show up, and then we left the little farm in Mongolia that had made so many people millionaires.

Bruce will be fine in Tennessee for about two months, and then he will start trying to figure out a way to go someplace, someplace exciting and profitable. I am almost the same way, but there will never be another place like China, Mongolia and Russia that Bruce can go to, that will satisfy his urge to roam. My millions came to me because Bruce was not a selfish person.

This Is The End Of "A Gold Mine Up Near The Sky."

Author/Narrator: Larry English

This next story is fiction, it does not resemble any family that I know, but it does resemble famlies that I know of. Hard working, tax paying, God loving farmers. The back bone of this country.

Family Life Down On The Farm

OUR FARM IS THE BEST farm around here. It is rich land and we grow a bumper crop every year. Jeb, my brother and I, work our ass off on this farm and our pa will just give us a little bit of money, and promises to pay us later.

Last year he sold over a thousand bushel of corn and several truckloads of sweet potatoes. Me and Jeb got two hundred dollars each at the end of the year, just before he went on a vacation for three months; this was right after he sold thirty five head of cattle.

He does this every year, but usually he pays us fifteen hundred dollars each, that amounts to about fifty cents per hour for our work. Me and Jeb both know that this is not right, but he has always said that when he dies that the farm will be ours, and we believed him.

Recently our Pa, on two occasions, has talked about selling the farm, and we know that he will, and we know that he will completely leave us out in the cold with nothing, this is the kind of sorry ass hole that he is.

Our dad is fifty four years old, and he takes these long vacations every year. Every year when he comes home he has a new woman with him, the last one only stayed two months before she left, she said that Pa owed her over a thousand dollars, because he borrowed it from her to pay the motel bill. She worked in the restaurant there and slipped food out for both of them to eat. I knew that he was a sorry bastard, but I did not know that he would stoop that low.

My Ma run away with the neighbor when I was just two years old, and my Pa raised us, we were learnt to work on the farm and we were not learnt anything else, we both know how to make a farm pay off, we are both real good farmers.

Jeb never did go to school, our pa would not let him go, and he said that it was a waste of time, but the folks down at the court house raised so much hell about it, that by the time that I was old enough to go to school, Pa let me go. Jeb is two years older than I am and a lot smarter than me. Jeb can pick a guitar better than anyone that I have ever heard, and he can play a fiddle and a piano.

Five or six years ago, when Pa come home from one of his vacations, he brought home a really pretty woman with him. On the very first day that she was here, Jeb somehow wound up in the bed with her, and Pa caught them, he run them both off, but he let Jeb come back because there was a lot of work that needed to be done.

I know that this all sounds real bad, and I know that the neighbors talk about us, but the same thing has happened three times. Pa finds a girlfriend and brings her home, within the first two or three days, Jeb windes up with the girl, Pa runs them off, and then Jeb is back home within a week, but Pa stays pissed off for at least a month.

Jeb come up with this here idea, not me. I have finished high school and Jeb never went to school one day, but he is the smart one in this family. Pa is off on one of his vacations now, and Jeb said that when he comes back, that the three of us are going to set down and talk. We will have our way, or we will leave.

This farm is six hundred and sixty acres. Pa never bought any of it; it was given to him and our Ma, when Ma's Ma died. Now that our Pa has said that he may just sell the farm, we need to let him know that we want our part, and we want it now.

The high ground that we cleared off to grow beans on is just red dirt, and it is rocky and there are still some stumps on it, and Pa does not like that piece of land, but it is good for sweet potatoes and beans. We will tell him that we want that sixty acres for our own, thirty acres each, and we want it in our own name. And we will tell him that we will farm the other six hundred acres for him, cattle and all.

Jeb, with no education at all, is going up against Pa, and Pa has a college education, but no common horse sense, and that is what Jeb has plenty of.

Our plan was made; we both agreed with each other that we would stick with the plan, no matter what.

When Pa got home he was about half drunk so we waited a whole week for him to sober up. Instead of getting sober, he got drunker, so we told him that we needed to talk and he said okay. He agreed with us about the sixty acres of land, and it being transferred into our name. That is what we thought he would not agree with, but he did. Jeb and I both believed that if he had of been sober he would have fought us on this.

Pa had demands of his own. He was going to do the paper work on the transfer of the deeds; it was going to be done his way, and not our way. Not only that, but he wanted a signed contract from both of us that we were to run the farm for him, and we agreed to do that.

Jeb and I both were working, and Pa went to town to do the paper work. Me and Jeb were to get thirty acres each, a total of sixty acres, but Pa told them wrong and we each got sixty acres.

About a month later, the papers were mailed to us. I read them and told Jeb what it said. Jeb said to just let it be, Pa will never know the difference, because it does not look like he is ever going to sober up. That was two years ago, we still have the sixty acres each, and Pa is still drunk.

Me and Jeb are now getting ready to plant, we plow from daylight until it gets too dark to see, and if it is a full moon we both plow as long as we can walk.

With all of this work to be done it looks like Pa would help us, but he does not. Tomorrow we will plant corn in the bottom land by the creek, and Saturday we will plant pole beans on part of our own acres.

Our Pa gets mad when he sees Jeb or me working on our own land, but we take one day each week and do our work, so that we will have something to sell.

We both worked for fifty straight days until everything was planted, then it rained for two days, a slow, gentle rain. In just two or three days we could see the corn and beans acoming up, that is a beautiful sight, and it makes for another bumper crop. Me and Jeb took a chance and set out forty acres of sweet potato slips, now we have to get out and find a buyer for a lot of sweet potatoes. We drove Pa's truck to Gordonville to the big packing plant there, and the manager told us that he would buy all of them if we promised all of them to him. We found out that a new packaging plant was opening up, and sweet potatoes were one of the main items that they wanted.

Jeb said that he could remember neighbors talking about our Pa, and how he was raised up. They said that he was as good of a feller as there ever was until he went off to college. When he come back home, he was not worth a shit, and he still ain't. Before Ma run off, he stole corn from the crib and sold it to buy whiskey. He was always bringing girls home and sleeping with them. Our Pa is about as low down of a scoundrel as you could ever find.

I think that we have got him by the balls now, because even if he sold the farm, me and Jeb owns the one hundred and twenty acres, sixty acres each, and he is the one that transferred the title over to us.

We are now going to try and help Pa get straightened out, get him sober, and force him to start working again. He ran this farm for years and it made money, until he got to drinking too much and screwing around with all of those girls in town, now he don't do nothing.

Me and Jeb can run this place, but he took all of the money and spent it. We had to sell hogs and cows to get the money to buy our seed and fertilizer.

Jeb plays the guitar for the band at the school square dance every Saturday night. He makes twenty five dollars, every week, for doing this, and that is the money that we have to spend.

These people that Pa is selling whiskey for got him in a lot of trouble just two weeks ago. He got caught with six gallons of corn whiskey out there in town. He was arrested and put in jail, me and Jeb went out there and got him out of jail, but then the judge said that he had to go to court next month. Pa was real scared, he was afraid that they would take the farm away from him, so he got the attorney to put the farm in Jeb's name, so that they could not take it from him. Pa thought that Jeb was not smart enough to know anything about the law and Pa would change the farm back into his name, after he went to court and everything was settled and he was cleared.

Now, Pa's part of the farm is in Jeb's name. Pa got one year in prison for transporting illegal alcohol beverage with intent to sell. If he had not been caught he would have made ten dollars. He made ten dollars per each case of six gallons that he sold. Not only that but he lost the truck, and that was the only way that we had to haul our farm supplies.

Jeb rode the mule to town and went to the courthouse and ask to speak to the judge. He told the judge that we needed the truck to earn a living, and the judge gave the old truck back to us. Everyone in the county knew how sorry our Pa was, and they knew mine and Jeb's situation, we both worked hard, and wanted no trouble of any kind.

As of right now, me and Jeb owns the whole farm. Our first job is to go back to Gordonville and try to make a deal with the packing house to buy everything that we grow. Our planting is over with for this year, but we can grow whatever they want us to for next year.

Our trip to the packing house paid off for us. They agreed to buy our entire crop, but next year they want us to grow cucumbers and sweet potatoes on all of the land that we have.

When Pa gets out of prison, Jeb said that we are going to be extra nice to him, our first crop will be sold by then, and we will give him forty dollars every week to live on, that is a hell of a lot more than he ever paid us. My room in the barn is all fixed up now and he can sleep out there. If he misses a day of work we will deduct eight dollars from his pay. If he drinks whiskey while here on the farm we will have to fire him. If he does not do any of these things, we will give him five hundred dollars at the end of the year.

Jeb told me to write these things down on paper, and as soon as Pa gets here we will have him to sign the paper. That way everybody knows how it is going to be.

Pa sold off thirty five cows before he left, but we have twenty four more cows and four bulls. We intend to sell half of the cows and keep all of the bulls, and all of the male calves. We will just raise some for beef to sell at the cattle sale. Not too far in the future we will be out of the cattle business because they eat too much.

Jeb went to town and tried to trade cows for a tractor. We ain't ever had no tractor and don't know exactly what kind we need, but Jeb told them that he would find out and then he would be back.

The hay that was in the barn loft is almost gone; we are cleaning out the last of it this week. Under all of that hay we found a wooden box with cash money in it. Twenty nine hundred dollars, all of it was fifty dollar bills. This is the money for the thirty five cows that Pa sold; the bill of sale was in the box with the money.

Jeb went back to the tractor store and paid twenty five hundred dollars and ten cows for a farm all tractor and a wagon and three attachments. The tractor had been used, but very little.

This was all put in my name, I signed the papers on it just like I did on the farm, but the farm is in both Jeb and my name. If Pa quits drinking and running women, we will put his name on there too, after three or four years goes by. Pa would have been okay if he had not gone to college, that's where he learnt all of those bad habits.

That first year that Jeb and me ran the farm, we sold thirty one truckloads of sweet potatoes off of our original land, one hundred and twenty acres.

The other part of the land produced four hundred bushel of corn, and a super market bought it in the field. We grew what we eat, and fed the animals on the farm, mules and cattle and a few chickens.

Our Pa got out of jail last Monday morning. We knew that he was getting out early because the judge told us about two weeks ago, and we were both glad to hear that good news. This is Wednesday and we have heard nothing from Pa yet.

In a tavern, in town, we found Pa. He was drinking and had a pretty women with him, I had never seen her before and do not think that she was a prostitute. He has only been out for two days, how he got tangled up with her, I do not know.

We took our Pa home and he settled down in his room, attached to the barn, and his lady friend went with him, they both come into the house to eat, and some time she does the cooking. I told Jeb to stay away from her and he said that he would.

Pa just will not work. He just wants to eat and lay around the room with his lady, he went to the court house in town and told the judge that he has no money, no home to live in, and because he has a record he cannot find a job. The judge helped him get food stamps and a check every month, now I know that he will not work. I told Pa that he had to move out of the barn unless he works, he said that he did not care if we kicked him out of the room, that the welfare would get him a better place to live. He seems to have it a lot better than me and Jeb.

We found out that Pa and his friend got out of jail on the same day, so they have been buddied up ever since then. They are both on welfare and both draw food stamps and a check, Pa told me and Jeb that they would take his check away from him if he worked any, so he won't work.

Jeb has said that when planting time comes that we both have to work sixteen hours every day, each one of us. But at the end of the year we will buy another tractor and we are going to plant every inch of this farm. He also said that were getting rid of the mules and all of the cattle except one cow for milk.

On Saturday nights Jeb has to leave early and go down to the square dance in town, he makes twenty five dollars for doing that, and he is only there for three hours. I have been there and I saw what Jeb goes for. She is a short little blond headed girl and she is really after Jeb, I'll bet anything that Jeb brings her home with him pretty soon.

When Pa and his friend were staying in the barn, I found out that Jeb was going there when Pa was gone someplace. When Pa found out, that is when they left and moved to town. If Jeb had any learning at all he would not do his Pa that way.

Just like I thought, Jeb married that little blond headed hussy and they moved into the room next to me. The first few nights was noisy, but it is okay now. She gets up when he does and she fixes all of our breakfast then she goes to work when jeb does, and works with him until quitting time.

I have been talking to the lady down there at the feed store, I did not ask her for a date, but she asks me if I had a girlfriend. Jeb was there and heard her say that, he said that she was hot for me, I don't know how he could tell just by that, but that's what he said.

It is time now to get the land ready to plant. We have got to turn it, then disc it up, and then lay it off, we can't plant for a month yet but we must be ready when the time comes.

Yesterday was Sunday, and we were all out there working and the preacher come by. He stopped and walked out to the field where we were and asks us if we did not know that this was the Lords day. This is Sunday. You should not be doing this on Sunday.

None of us knew that it was Sunday. But none of us knew that it was the Lords day either. None of us had ever been to church, but when that preacher left there, we knew. We promised the preacher that we would go to church the next week.

All three of us had nothing to wear, but work clothes. We drove all the way to Gordonville and found a store that sold clothes. A man named Will owned it, and he named the store Good Will. We all bought dress clothes and when we went home we each had two sets of clothes, so that we did not have to wear the same thing every time that we went someplace.

During the next week that preacher showed up at our house two times, and it was always right at going to work time. He would eat a biscuit and have some coffee and then say "let's do some work". He worked with us until noon and then went home. While he was there he told us that it was people like us that made a church, we were the kind of people that God wanted, and that we needed God, so be there Sunday morning at ten 0 clock. That preacher had gone out of his way to make friends with us and he showed us that he was not afraid of hard work. We planned our work so that we could be off on Sundays, so that we could be in church.

The first person that we saw on that Sunday morning was the lady from the feed store. She come to us and set with us all thorough Sunday school and church. I saw her every night for two weeks and then the preacher married us, now all four of us live in the same house.

We saw Pa and talked to him, we offered him the room to live in, and told him that he could work with us and that we would pay him. He said no, I have a better deal here where I am. The welfare pays my rent, gives me money to live on, and if I run out of wood for the heater, they pay for someone to bring me more, not only that, but I go to the Doctor or hospital for free. This is the best that I have ever had it, and I ain't going to screw it up now.

Jeb, not knowing no better, went and got his wife pregnant the first month that they were married. His wife is the hardest working women that I have ever seen, and she can lay those rows off just as straight as any man can, and that makes them easy to plant, and easy to harvest.

Me and Jeb both believe that by the end of this growing season that we will be able to buy another tractor, and be able to pay for it. If we can do that, it will really be something.

My wife that youst to work in the feed store had eleven brothers and three sisters and a Mother and Daddy; she did the cooking for all of them. Everyone in that family had a job to do; hers was to cook and milk two cows and take care of the milk. She is the best cook that I have ever seen, and because they grew a lot of sweet potatoes, she could show all of us ways to fix sweet potatoes that were different and very tasty. Sweet potato fries, sweet potato patties, mashed, tots, pies, and baked, and a few more ways to cook a sweet potato. Her mama and her grand ma was good cooks to. All of the neighbors bought sweet potato pies from them. Their land was so poor that it wouldn't grow nothing but sweet potatoes.

Most of our land is rich and fertile, but the high ground is not. It is red and rocky and poor, but it will grow beans and sweet potatoes, and that is about all.

In the spring of nineteen forty eight, it got real cloudy and stayed that way for four or five days. We had most of the planting done, all of the bottom land was planted in corn and it was up knee high, we was planting corn field beans in with the corn when it commenced to rain. The first day of rain it was soft and easy, just like we wanted, then that night it started raining like none of us had ever seen before. We layed there in the bed and listened to that downpour, we knowed that our crop was gone, and that it may be too late to replant.

When it got daylight we were all outside looking at the mess that we had. Our rich and fertile top soil was washed down stream to the lake that was a mile down below us. What we had left there was ground that is hard, and rocky with boulders sticking up that was as big as a car. If we could ever plow this land and make it soft enough to plant, it would be a miracle, and then it may not even grow a bean or a sweet potato.

Our best milk cow had washed away also, almost all of the chickens were gone, and some of the ones that had enough sense get up in a tree were still here.

The foot log that we had used to cross the creek to get to the pasture, ever since I can remember, it is gone too, so is the toilet, even the hole is gone.

We have had bumper crops for several years. There is enough can stuff in the pantry to last us for a year, we have corn in the crib, that we can grind up for bread, and to feed the animals. We lost our top soil but we still have more than most people.

The small flood that we had, wiped out the new packing house that was buying all of our produce. The owners had to file for bankruptcy so there will not be anyone to buy what we grow.

Jeb said that if the tractors will break up that hard ground that we have down there where the top soil washed away, that we will be okay and as soon as it dries out some, we will start working on it.

The ground was dry and hard, but by going over it twice, with a turning plow, it was workable. We plowed around the boulders and the real rocky places and eventually this land was much better than I ever thought that it would be.

Everyone that we knew was hit as hard as we were by the flood, but we were the only ones that bounced back like we did, this is because me and Jeb both married farm girls that were uset to hard work and our Pa was so hard on us growing up, and made us work hard.

Planting season was over with. The sweet potato plants that the feed store had left over was going to be thrown out, so they gave all of them to us and there were several cases of them.

Me and Jeb worked day and night to get the ground ready to plant the sweet potato slips and then all four of us spent one week down on our knees setting out the slips, and when we finished there was thirty five acres of sweet potatoes planted and not one potato was sold yet.

My wife was the expert on cooking sweet potatoes. Jeb put her in charge of that, if we ever got any potatoes to cook.

The high ground was not ruined by the flood, and the plants were growing good up there.

Jeb went to Gordonville looking for a company to build a processing plant to clean and cook the potatoes and then to package them and store them in a walk in cooler until sold. He found a company to do this, but it cost almost two hundred thousand dollars. I am not sure that Jeb realized how much money that was, but anyway he made the deal, knowing that I would agree with what he said, and I did agree.

Jeb signed a contract letting the six hundred acres that was Pa's part of the land, stand good for the construction and completion of the whole project. The contract included a steam boiler to cook the potatoes with steam. If we lost this and could not pay the debt off, we would still have our one hundred and twenty acres, Jeb made a bold move, risky but bold.

Within a month the company moved in with dozers and equipment, Jeb was there telling them where to place the buildings and each part of the operation. He put it all on our part of the land and on the highest point so that no water could ever get to it.

The one hundred and twenty acres of sweet potatoes, on the high ground, were doing great, and it would be a big push in the right direction if we could get that much product on the market, to start us off.

The papers were all signed, Jeb's and my signature both were there and we had promised to pay off two hundred thousand dollars plus interest in three years, in three equal payments, or they get the farm.

We just set back and watched them taters grow, and grow they did. It was the best crop that we had ever grown, we harvested wagon load after wagon load. After the potatoes had dried for about two weeks, we started the process of cleaning and cooking them. Cindy, my wife, was in charge of the processing plant, what she told us to do, we done. She knew everything there was to know about a sweet potato.

I had known all the time that it would be my job to get out and sell, and now the time had come to do just that. Jeb told me that grocery stores was the place to sell to, and don't go to some horses ass in the store that don't have no power, go to the top dog, wherever he or she is, the owner if you can find them.

I was not sure that our old truck would make the trip, but I drove to the nearest chain store. I found out that that chain of stores had sixty five stores and the main office was in Claxton, some of the stores were in other states.

I talked to the manager of all of the produce that went into the sixty five stores and he was interested but had to see some of our product. I called Cindy and she told me that she would have the packages ready in three days, so I drove home to get them.

Our new plant had hot water, electricity, a bath room and a telephone; our house did not have any of that.

On the way out of Claxton I saw a sign that said "meat and produce distributor". I pulled in to the office and made a deal with them to pick up our product and sell it to the grocery stores, if our place that we prepared the product in, passed the health department inspection, and I knew that it would.

When I gave the produce buyer the packages, of sweet potato fries, patties, and pie filler, he liked it, and immediately gave me the okay and a letter of approval. I gave the distributor a copy of the letter, they told me to call them when we are ready. When Cindy says we are ready, we are in business.

Down in the bottom, in that poor ass dirt that is full of rocks, the plants are growing like crazy, that is good because it takes over three months for sweet potatoes to grow and form the tuber.

That dam Jeb has always been a womanizer, but now I have caught him with the only hired girl that we have. I walked in on them and they were kissing. They were fully clothed and presentable, but Jeb was wrong, he was a married man. and she knew it. She still works for us, and is a good worker. Jeb's wife knows about it and she is still here too.

Berners's meat and produce distributers picked up their first load, from us, this morning, and this way of selling is good, they buy from us, and then resell.

The first one hundred and twenty acres of sweet potatoes has been harvested, dried, processed and sold. Business is good. We received pay for everything just like they said we would.

Jeb had bought a tractor that plowed up the sweet potatoes and they were mostly on top of the ground, then another tractor picked them up, after the vines had been cut away.

Jeb and his wife have a new baby, and his girlfriend is pregnant now also, he may have a problem.

When the potatoes on the bottom land, if they produce the same as they always have, are harvested, we will be able to make our first yearly payment.

Three years went by fast, and at the end of the fourth year the processing plant was all paid for, plus we had bought a new ford truck.

We, our family is in the money, but neighbors still look down on us because of the way that our Pa was, and because of Jeb's wanting to date every woman that he sees. He keeps two women happy now, and still goes to town on Saturday nights, looking.

I guess that it must be in the blood for Jeb to be like he is. Our grand ma, on Ma's side, was a rounder also; I can't believe some of the tales that I have heard about her. She shot grandpa when they were young, just because he was in swimming with two women, and she had several men friends that came to see her, regularly. Grandpa still had lead in his leg when he died. Grandma got married two times after he died.

Our Pa's Pa was a horse trader, and a preacher. His reputation is worse than any of the rest of the family. He was married seven times and divorced seven times, always keeping whatever money and property that they had between him and his wife; he was a shyster preacher, and a fast talker.

Last Saturday night, Jeb went to town just like he always did, except on Sunday morning he was not home so me and my wife went on to church without him. One of the members said to me that he was sorry about Jeb getting shot, he never knowed that we did not know about it. We left the church then and went to the hospital to see about Jeb. Jeb was not there, he was at the morgue. A man caught Jeb out in the parking lot with his wife and he shot and killed him.

The sheriff did not even arrest the man, he said that Jeb had got by with more in the past few years than he should have, and should have been shot a long time ago. He was lucky that he lived as long as he did.

The woman was arrested for fornication, but her husband bailed her out of jail, and took her home.

Our family never did have a graveyard before, but now we have started one up on the hill above the barn. Jeb cleared that spot out to build them a new house, but that did not work out, so now Jeb is there where he can oversee everything that goes on, here on this farm.

Our Pa was there at the funeral, he told all of the members of our family that Jeb should have been ashamed of himself for running around on his wife, that was just no way for a married man to do. No one mentioned to him that he did the same thing.

Now I have got to train all three of the women to run the tractors. Jeb's wife, and Jeb's friend, will have to farm the sixty acres of high ground that they have, for that is their profit to have to live on.

Last winter me and Jeb built an addition on to the barn and we built a parking cover for five vehicles. We had made arrangements to buy another tractor, and that gives us four tractors. We each have our own tractor to work with. Six hundred and sixty acres is a lot of plowing, planting, and harvesting. Jeb's friend owns nothing here, but she is one of the family, and she does as much work as any of us.

Our neighbors still talk about us and the way we live. Since Jeb died, there are three ladies and just one man that live here. They talk about that, and then there is our system of our finances. We do things our way, not like other people do. When our money comes in, it goes into the bank. Each of us gets fifty dollars every week. In ten years we have bought four tractors and a truck, but we owe for one tractor and will pay for it next fall.

This farm is a money maker, but we all have to work all day every day, and we do. Jeb always said not to worry about what other people said, just do what you want to, and never owe any of your neighbors any money or a favor, but help them if you can.

Now, twenty years after the flood that nearly wiped us out, we can look back and see our good times and our bad times. Losing Jeb was a heart breaking experience for all of us, but we recovered. We still have Jeb's wife and friend, and three children. Those children all are good dirt farmers and run the tractors from daylight till dark with no complaints. They have all completed high school and their college is paid for if they will go, but they will not go, they want to farm.

Five years ago I bought Jeb's part of the farm and paid his wife for it. She took the money and built a nice house up on top of the hill by the two big oak trees. Then after that I built us a house up there close to it. We are still close together, that's the way we want it.

After all of the building was paid for, we still had almost seven hundred thousand dollars in the bank.

Like my Pa, I never bought the land either. But the way that it turned out, I am the one that is here to manage it, and I have done the best that I could. There are seven of us in this family and that money in the bank is to take care of us, while we are here. Someday the money and land will be divided equally between all of our family, or at least that is the way that I want it to be.

Jeb's wife had two babies with Jeb and then after Jeb was gone, she remarried and had two more, and all four of them wuz boys. Me and my wife have three and that makes a total of ten people that depend on this farm for our living. Seven children to be schooled.

We can make it okay because we now have five tractors to farm with, when a boy is twelve years old he can run a tractor as good as anybody but can only work about eight or nine hours a day, he is not strong enough to work all day like a man does.

The fifty acres just south of us is being auctioned off next week because the owners did not make the bank payments, we have a chance to buy it from the bank, and we have the money to pay for it. Tonight our family will discuss it and make the decision, weather to buy it or not. If there is one person that votes no, we will not buy that land. If everyone votes yes, we will buy it. This is the way that our family does things, and we do not care what other folks think about our system.

We have a stream of water that runs through our farm, and it originates on that fifty acres. Three large springs make up our creek and that is the main reason that I want to buy the land, but it is still up to the family to make that decision.

Now that I am in my seventys, and those young boys that I learnt how to run the tractors and to plant the crops, and to harvest and sell and to take care of the money, they are in their twentys and thirtys now. I know that they will run this farm the right way, and not make the same mistakes that my pa made.

The family went and done it. They voted to buy the fifty acres that lays just south of us. They voted to get it cleared as soon as possible and to have it ready to plant by the coming season. Fifty more acres of sweet potatoes means that the processing plant will have to be enlarged, and they voted to do that also. And they voted to retire my wife and me both. We both will receive pay for the rest of our lives, sixty dollars each, every week.

I guess that this will give our neighbors something else to talk about, but I still wish that pa was here to see what all we have done.

These kids are smart and they can run this place without me and Ma, but we are still going to work some weither they like it or not. We aim to farm the fifty acres that they just bought, for the family to farm.

Jeb's wife Liz and her four boys want to work with us, but I want the two boys, that Liz had in her second marriage to work with me, and Jeb's and Liz's two to work on the other acres. I have things to show those boys about farming that they need to know. I have already taught the others the same thing.

What my family has done, they have done, and it's all over with and there ain't no way to change that, but we have all lived good and have always had plenty to eat. I just hope that the future is as good as the past has been.

End Of The Story

Author And Narrator Larry English

The Adventures Of Alvin

THIS STORY IS FICTION, BUT IT IS INSPIRED BY THE LIFE OF A REAL PERSON.

THIS IS A STORY ABOUT a gentle gentleman, an easy going, accommodating, and very friendly man that would do you a favor in a heartbeat. That is, if you do not do him or his family any harm in any way, then he is hell on wheels. If he is mad at you for any reason, you better leave town. He made big bad Leroy Brown look like a Sunday School teacher.

His father was born near lake Okeechobee Florida in 1891, and managed to make a living from this huge lake by selling fish, alligators and frogs. Alvin was born on a houseboat on this twenty eight thousand square mile lake and lived there most of his young life. Naturally, he knew where every tree and bush was. He knew where every lilly pad was, and every canal, island, marker and sunken boat. He seemed to know the top of the water and the bottom also, he was amazing, and he was my friend. Alvin taught me how to build fish traps, and how to cut trails thorough heavy peppergrass, and how to place the traps in the trails so that they would catch the most fish. He was not a selfish person.

One thing he did not like, and that was game wardens. The first two times that I went out on the lake with Alvin, the game warden tied to stop us, Alvin would not stop and we were chased, but not caught. It was very important for Alvin to have the fastest boat in lake Okeechobee, or any place near lake Okeechobee.

I ask Alvin one time to help me get a boat and motor just like he had, and he did. The same person built both boats for us and they were just alike, and they both had one hundred and fifty horsepower Mercury motors. The day after I got my boat, Alvin traded for a one hundred and seventy five horsepower mercury motor for his boat.

Alvin is a legend around this lake; you can hear all sorts of stories about him. Some may not be true, but I know for certain that some of the meanest and daring ones are, as a matter of fact, true.

One night my wife and I were in one airboat and Alvin was in an airboat by himself. He wanted my wife to see how he caught alligators, Alvin had already told me about his plan. We left the house there in Lakeport just after dark, and traveled about six miles out to the point of a reef, there we stopped and looked all around with our headlights. Several gators were just laying out there in the moonlight and we could hear them grunting at each other. I had been instructed to stay close to his boat, but by no means to let my headlight shine in his face. I followed Alvin's instructions and when he let his boat drift up to this huge gator, even I knew that it was way too big for any one man to catch. I was not over five feet from Alvin's boat, with my headlight off, when he reached down into the dark, snake infested water of lake Okeechobee and grabbed an eight or ten-foot alligator by the lips. He managed to drag that monster into his boat, and then when he saw how big it really was he could not let it go. Alvin had both arms and both legs around that gator, but after wrestling for a few minutes it overpowered Alvin and got loose. While lying on his back in the floor of his airboat, Alvin kicked the gator back into the water. In a few minutes, after he regained his composure he just said, "I decided to let that one go".

For a couple of years right after we first met Alvin, he would occasionally come by our house and give us a half of a hog, or a quarter of a beef. He told us that some of his Indian friends had more than they needed and had given it to him. We did not believe that, but we never knew what to expect out of Alvin. Much later we found out that he would go into the woods at night and kill and dress a beef or a hog, what ever he came upon. He had a steady group of customers that bought fish every Saturday morning, and they bought beef and pork also, and of course at a discounted price.

A few times I would luck up and have a really good catch of specks [called Crappy in some parts of the country]. When I did Alvin would come in with twice that amount. No way could he be out fished. One time I caught fourteen hundred pounds and knew that I had Alvin James beat. But Alvin caught eleven hundred pounds in the morning and that afternoon he caught thirteen hundred pounds. I had to weigh mine and sell them for fifty five cents per pound with a tag on each fish. Alvin sold his for one dollar per pound with no tags, to his regular customers.

There are many tales around about Mr. James and some are true, but not all of them. For example, I was told by a fisherman that lived in Okeechobee, that he saw Alvin shoot the pilot of a small air plane that had landed on the dike near Sportsman Village, and take a briefcase out of the plane. At the time Alvin was supposed to be doing this, he was fishing with me and two of my relatives.

This story I know is not true. Plus, I never did hear of a plane and it's dead pilot being found, there on the dike. Because of Alvin's popularity many such stories have been rumored.

Another tall story is the one that circulated all around this area about Alvin being in a houseboat and airplanes flying over and dropping dope to him on lake Okeechobee. No way.

The one about Alvin living with his friend's wife may or may not be true. I do not know. But the part about Alvin holding his girl friend's husband prisoner, for several weeks, while he was staying with her, I do not believe. Alvin was Strong enough and mean enough to do this, but he was good enough and fair enough so that he did not have to do this. I fished with Alvin a lot and I gator hunted with him many times and I would have known about some of these things if it had happened.

One time Alvin and I were out on the lake at night running traps on a full moon. It was light enough so that we could find the traps, dump them, separate the fish and return the traps to the water without a light. Alvin saw a twelve-inch alligator there beside a grass patch and caught it; we put it into a sack to take home. In a few minutes he caught another one. Before we went home that night Alvin had caught thirty gators all about the same size. The only reason he stopped catching them was the sack got full and there was not another sack in the boat. Early the next morning Alvin went out and sold the gators for three dollars each. He also sold the specs that he got from the traps for one dollar per pound, that night Alvin made three hundred and ninety dollars. His cost was zero, with the exception of a couple gallons of gasoline.

For me it was an education, the same as when we went hunting or just airboat riding. Sometimes we went hog hunting in the airboat at night. Alvin would shoot the hogs right between the eyes and within fifteen minutes they were skinned, gutted with the head off and we were gone. I had never experienced these things before, I had not even thought about these things before, and if anyone told me that they had done these things, I would have thought they were lying.

One time I was with Alvin and we were running his fish traps. It was late afternoon and Alvin had about two hundred pounds of large specs. As we were on the way back to the boat landing there were two black men and two black ladies fishing. Alvin pulled up beside them and asks if they were having any luck and they said no. Alvin sold them two hundred pounds of fish for one hundred dollars. Before we got to the boat landing Alvin dumped six more traps and got another hundred pounds of fish. He had traps in trails from Indian Prairie canal to Clewiston, which is about fifteen or twenty miles. Like I said before, Alvin was amazing. I had a good job and a small business and Alvin made more money each week than I did.

For a few months I was there living in our mobile home so that I could run traps in the daytime. One night just after dark Alvin came and set there with me and we watched TV a while, then he asks if I wanted to ride some. I thought he meant in the airboat, I said yes. We got in his pick up and drove to Okeechobee to a bar that had a lot of black people around it. Alvin reached in the back of his truck and got a garbage bag full of something and carried it into the bar. He later told me that it was marijuana, if it was or not I do not know. But while Alvin was in that bar, I was setting there in his truck at night in the parking lot of a black bar. When he returned he asks if I was nervous at all, and I said "yes", he moved a towel that was there in the seat beside him and there was a three fifty seven pistol under the towel. Then he told me that no one there at that place would bother him or anyone that was with him, and he could guarantee that.

One time my wife and I was in my fishing boat and Alvin was in his fishing boat. We were going down the big canal from Clewiston to near Lakeport where the canal went back into the lake. Ahead we could see a large yacht meeting us and a wake of water about twenty feet high was in front of the big boat. My wife and I were in front of Alvin. We stopped because I was afraid of the big wave. Alvin came along side of us and asks what was wrong, when I told him, he laughed at me. He said follow me. We did, and as we come to the wall of water we just rode up about twenty feet, real smooth and down the other side, that was another first for me. There was a time there that I could not see Alvin or his boat, but that was nothing to him, he had been there and done that before.

Alvin really did know people in high places. I have been with him several times when a jet plane would buzz our area that we lived in, and we may be on the lake fishing or just setting at the house, but Alvin would get in a hurry and leave fast. There was a landing strip five miles from our house and the small jet would land. They, whoever was in the plane, had come after Alvin. Sometime they were gone one day and sometime a week. I assume that it was the same people, or group of people, that owned the plane and owned a lot of land there in the area. Alvin was supposedly on their payroll as a lubricating engineer. I do know for sure that Alvin was the fishing guide and hunting guide for that group. When none of that group was in the area I went into the hunting camps and the water holes where they feed the deer, turkeys and wild hogs, but I never did kill anything, I was not hunting, I was just looking. I also know for sure that the person that Alvin had out fishing, on more than one occasion, had their lunch brought to them, delivered from Tampa, by jet.

One night there on Lake Okeechobee, the water was low. A lot of the shallow water area was just grass. Some places had soupy mud and at night it was just perfect for air boating. Alvin came to our house and said he knew where we might be able to kill a deer if we wanted to go. We were always ready to go when Alvin planned something like this. Alvin knew my brother in law better than he did me; I had met Alvin thorough Ralph. We went out on the grass flats and there were dozens of cows there. We had two airboats, Alvin was in one and two of my brothers in law and I was in the other one. We slid around thorough the cows looking for deer but found none. Then all of a sudden a huge bobcat jumped up and ran out thorough the grass. Alvin ran after the big cat and when he got to it he turned the airboat on the side and slid over it sideways, mashing the cat down into the mud. The cat came up ready to fight, all bowed up in the back and looking for something to attack. Alvin ran over the cat again then killed it with the boat paddle. Like I said before you never knew what to expect when you went with Alvin.

A friend of Alvin's had a small plane and the two of them would fly around over the lake and look for shell cracker beds. They decided to go up to the North Carolina Mountains and look at the mountains from above. Since I knew that area they asks me if I wanted to go, so I did. We landed in Franklin, NC. We got a car at the airport and drove into town to eat. A big bad looking cloud come rolling across the mountains and the pilot said that we better get out of here that it may storm for several days, because this time of year it does that sometime. We left as soon as the gas tanks were topped off. Instead of running out of the storm we ran into it. I recognized where we were, it was a place that I had lived in at one time. We got down to 300 feet trying to land but there was no place to set the plane down. We were in a terrible storm. Water was coming in thorough the small air vent adjusters. At times we were totally out of control, the tail of the plane was in front in the direction we were moving. The propeller of the plane was bending and the pilot said that the plane would stay together if he could keep it right side up, but upside down the plane may break up.

Lightning knocked out some of the instruments. The next time I saw the ground was when the pilot said, "there is the airport". He had seen it on the map but we could not find it. He started to land and we were not over thirty feet from the ground when he pulled up as fast as he could. This was a racetrack. He got back up to five hundred feet and then saw the airport and we landed safely.

The mechanics at the airport said they could not believe that we come in from the north, no plane could fly in the storm that they had the reports of, but we did. The mechanics replaced some fuses and Alvin and the pilot was ready to fly back to Fla. I refused to get back on the plane. I told them to go on that I would be there the next day on the bus, but they would not do that. We stayed there in that Georgia town just about sixty miles south of Franklin NC. That is one time that Alvin was not in full control.

My brother in law had a forty-foot houseboat there on his property. I had a mobile home on the other side of his property. While I was staying there to run traps, Alvin knocked on my door at two a m in the morning, and said that Ralph had told him he could use the houseboat for a while and they would be quite. All I wanted was to go back to sleep. I never heard anything else that night, but three or four days later I was fishing from the bow of the houseboat and I saw thorough the front window eight or nine bags of stuff like Alvin delivered to Okeechobee.

I went over to my mobile home and closed it up and then drove to Tampa. I did not want to be there near that stuff. A few days later when I went back, and the bags were gone. I never did mention it to Ralph, or Alvin. Ralph had the boat secured with a log chain and a huge lock, welded to a large concrete foundation that had been made for this purpose. But, Alvin had the key to the cabin door. I knew that on certain occasions Alvin would use the boat to party.

One time I was going hunting with two young men that I commercial fished with. They were brothers and both of them had trail bikes. They hog hunted on the bikes. I had heard about this several times and finally I was invited to go with them, and I gladly accepted. They ran the hogs down on the bikes and caught them. Then they carried them home and put them into a pen and would feed them corn for a few weeks, then sold them or eat them.

On this trip things worked different. I was on the bike behind the youngest of the brothers. We were a mile or so into the woods on a sand road traveling approximately twenty miles an hour. We rounded a sharp curve and there in the road was four or five pick up trucks and a game warden vehicle, a large horse trailer and five or six men, they were loading the black bags onto the horse trailer. Both brothers opened the bikes wide open; both bikes had the front wheel off of the ground. I looked over the shoulder of my driver and the speed ometer read sixty five, which is fast on a sand road. The trucks came after us but we outran them and got away. We were out of hearing from them but they come straight to us. We out ran them again and the same thing happened. It could only be one thing. A plane was spotting us and guiding the men in the trucks to us. We turned the motors off and listened. We were right, a small plane was up there very high and after we figured this out we put the bikes under thick trees and ran on foot, staying off of the road. We went thorough palmettos and ditches full of water, but no one got snake bit. After we walked a few miles we heard a truck coming with the radio on real loud, we were hid but we could see the road. We knew who this was so we let them see us.

Alvin had a scanner in his truck. He listened to the plane guiding the trucks to us, then he got these young kids to drive out this road and pick us up, he knew we were out there. We knew what would happen to us if we were caught. Others had been in our situation and did not get away, but would be found later.

The black plastic bags were worth several million dollars. Everyone there in that group of men would make more money than you could earn on a job in a lifetime.

These people would not hesitate to kill in order to protect that kind of money.

In this small town there were six people that controlled that part of the county. The law and the state game warden was involved. One of the largest business owners in the state, was the boss, and he and his family were already billionaires. But they were making more now than ever. They never did get caught as a group, but one or two individuals did get caught and never did tell on the others. Alvin was one of these.

An airplane, a huge D C three, would land on a grass strip in the swamps of South Fla. Horse trailers would be waiting to get their load, and then within one hour all of the bales of dope were gone. After many loads had been hauled this way, the trafficking started including diamonds and gold, from Columbia

This is when Alvin could not resist taking more than his part. On one particular airplane that was coming in to set down there, Alvin was setting the lights to guide the plane to the center of the strip for a safe landing, because it was mud on both sides and the plane could flip and crash. The plane landed safely and it was a little early, Alvin was there alone with just the two pilots. He knew what was on the plane. His job was to light the runway and pump one hundred gallons of gasoline into the planes tanks, that is all.

Alvin could not hear the trucks or see the lights from any of the trucks that were coming after their load. In the cockpit of the plane he saw a small suitcase that probably contained jewels and diamonds and gold. It was said that Alvin had to act fast, that he shot both of the pilots and grabbed the suitcase and ran.

One of the men he shot died but one lived to tell. No one knows what Alvin did with the suitcase, it was never found, that is, if he ever had it. The law was there days later, but all of the dope was gone and the plane was clean. The pilot told what Alvin did and they found a small amount of dope in Alvin's truck. Alvin got fifteen years in the federal prison, but they say he still got away with murder. I did not see any of this; it is all hear say.

I did not see or talk to Alvin for the next twelve or thirteen years. I talked to some of his family and I knew that he was sentenced to fifteen years. His high- powered friends in high places kept telling him that he would be out soon, and that he had a lot of money deposited in his account in Switzerland. None of this turned out to be true. I was told about this Switzerland account long before Alvin was in trouble. He, Alvin, had money going into that account for at least two years for the work he was doing for Mr. Big. Alvin told me that he would be a wealthy man when they quit the business, but he could not show any money now. Alvin lived in an old house, drove an old truck, and only spent the money he made fishing.

There were three of us there, with Alvin, when he talked about this. We were all good friends, and we all three believed what he told us.

One of the money makers that Alvin had, before the dope deal got started in a big way, was the gator skin sales. Alvin would skin the gators, roll the skins up as tight as he could get them, and tie them to keep them in a tight roll. Then place the skins into a barrel of brine. These barrels would be hauled to Louisiana and the skins sold for about ten dollars per lineal foot. Each barrel would contain as much as four hundred feet. Shoes, belts, jackets, hats etc; would be made from the gator skins.

Years later, after all of these things had happened, I went to Alvin's home for a visit. We were both older and it showed, of course. Alvin had been out of prison for almost two years. He was the same stocky built, wavy haired man that I remembered back when things were so good for both of us. Alvin could not do the things that he did back then, but he got a thrill just talking about what he had done. What he told me that day was the same thing he had told me years before, so I know it was the truth.

Alvin also told me the story about how and why he was sent to prison. How he was to get out very soon and how wealthy he would be as soon as he got out. The big shot with the jet plane sure did lie to Alvin, and it cost him the last fifteen or so years of his life.

That last visit with Alvin lasted about six or seven hours and it seemed like he wanted me to ask more questions. He wanted to talk about things that happened back then, because then he was the cock of the walk, he had all of the big connections, with the top people, he was the best fisherman around there and every one knew it. He was the fastest thing on the water and every one knew that. He was the best of the best, however, gambling was not his thing. I watched Alvin lose fifteen thousand dollars one afternoon, in a poker game that did not last over one hour. Alvin asks me to get a paper bag from under the seat of his truck. That bag had five thousand dollars in it and he lost that also. Then he put his truck up to stand good for a pot that five players had about six thousand dollars each in and he won that pot. Then he quit the game and went home. Later that night Alvin told me that, that was the last time that he would ever play poker. He admitted that he did not know how to gamble and he had tried bluffing but it did not work.

This is just some of the things that Alvin got involved in while I knew him. Alvin did not go to school very much, I do not think, but he was educated in a different

way.

Alvin could make a great living from the lake, he made more money, than I have ever made, and he never had a job.

Alvin was a ladies' man, this was his problem. His six foot two inch slender frame and his curly hair attracted the females to him, he was, as I have heard him called, a ladies man, and the meanest man in town. Alvin hung around a beer joint called the green hut, and it was a known fact that girls came from as far away as Fort Myers to try and date Alvin.

I did not know this about him for a long time. My only interest in Alvin was fishing, he was teaching my brother-in-law and me how to trap fish, because Alvin caught fish when no one else could.

Alvin had a beautiful wife, and when Alvin was at home she would not speak to another man. But when Alvin was away on one of his trips, his wife could be found at the green hut, during the early part of the night, then she would be gone someplace until the next morning. A lot of rumors was flying around about this and everyone around there knew that sooner or later there would be a killing, just as soon as Alvin found out who she was with.

Alvin did have a girlfriend, and he did stay at her house some of the time. Alvin did call her husband out of the house and beat him with a palmetto root until he was unconscious, then taking him to a cabin in the woods and holding him prisoner for two weeks, as I heard it. The man knew that Alvin would kill him if he told anyone, so he kept quiet and shared his wife with Alvin until his death, which was only about one year. She only lived less than a year after her husband's death. They both died from fear.

In the early months of nineteen seventy, a Judge was murdered there in Glades County, and his head was cut off, his head was found on the side of the road in a plastic bag. No one talked about this, it was very quiet, the papers reported it, but in one or two days it was forgotten about. Rumors did fly. It was rumored that This judge was in the dope business himself. It was also rumored that this judge made a threat that he was going to stop the drug business in this area. All kinds of rumors were heard, but they were just rumors.

We did not see Alvin every day, not even every week, just every once in a while when he decided to come by our house for a visit. But we noticed that Alvin had not been by to visit in a while. So, I went to his house to visit him, and was told that Alvin was gone someplace, and he had not been seen in quite a while, and I was told this in such a manner that I knew to not come back here no more.

Two weeks later, in the middle of the night, Alvin knocked on our door. He ask if we were all okay, and I told him yes. Then he told me that he was having to stay hid because of money problems. He said "I owe a lot of money and I can't pay", so I have to stay out of sight for a while. Alvin ask me to do him a favor. He said "if there is an emergency in my family, will you come after me?" No way could I refuse that kind of request from a friend.

The next morning Alvin took me to the place where he was hiding. Two miles in an air boat, then on an island between Lakeport and highway twenty seven, there was no town nearby. Alvin had a cabin there with heat, a bathroom, running water, from a well. It was all run by a generator. This cabin was on dry land, but was surrounded by water and there was another air boat tied up to his dock, but no kind of communitions. Alvin stayed here for over a year, and I was never ask to deliver a message to him.

Just before Christmas in nineteen seventy five, Alvin was in a very bad auto accident in Sebring, Florida. A drunk driver hit him from the rear. The drunk driver was killed, and Alvin was almost killed. He had five broken ribs, a fractured neck, and a broken leg, He was in the hospital for three months and was in a coma for two weeks.

While in a coma, Alvin said that he talked to God, Alvin says that God talked to me about every wrong and bad thing that I had ever done. I promised God that I would change, and that I would try to make things right with the people that I had offended.

As soon as Alvin got out of the hospital he went to the preacher and confessed his sins to him. The following Sunday Alvin went to the Alter and there and then he confessed to everyone about his sinful life, and he joined the Church. From that time on Alvin was in Church regularly.

Alvin lived the rest of his life as a good Christian man. He got out of prison three years before the auto accident.

This Is The End Of My Story About Alvin.

Author And Narrator Larry English.

Doyle Bradshaw

AS I SET HERE BY Doyle's grave, my mind flashes back to the days of his poverty, and his unbelievable rise in wealth,

Doyle Bradshaw and his sister lived in crossroad Ga., a small town up in the mountains near the Tennessee state line. When he was six years old, and his sister was four, their mother deserted her family and left with another man. Their father did take care of them until he died of alcohol poison, when Doyle was thirteen, this is when Doyle moved in with his uncle Dave and aunt Mary, and his sister dot was placed in a foster home over in Tennessee. All Doyle knew about his sister was that she lived with a nice family, that owned a grocery store in Cotton, Tennessee.

Uncle Dave and aunt Mary did not have a car, they were farmers so they had plenty of food, but there was no money, the only time any money come into the house, was when they sold a pig or a beef, and this is when they ordered shoes and clothes from the Sears catalog, this way the mail man brought it right to their mail box.

Doyle was always clean, but his cloths were ragged, his shoes were worn out, and needed half soles, you could hear the soles flop when he walked, and he always needed a haircut, and when he did get one his aunt cut it, and it was a bowl cut.

Everyone else in school went to parties and ball games but not Doyle, he rode the bus home every day and did his chores, and then he would study until midnight. They did not have electric lights, or water in the house, he studied by kerosene lamps, on written test Doyle would make a perfect score, but if he was ask a question in class he would say 'I don't know', he just would not speak out in class.

Doyle was like this all thorough high school. When we were in the tenth grade I was going fishing with my uncle Claude, and as we went by where they lived I saw him out in the front of the house, I got Claude to stop and I ask Doyle if he wanted to go fishing, he said okay. To my surprise he got into the truck with us and we went to the river fishing. Later in the day I found out that was the only time that he had ever been fishing in his life.

Our senior year in school the FFA arranged for a busload of students to go to Atlanta to the state fair, to attend the farm shows. The future farmers of America had cattle shows, and prize hogs and it was free for us to see.

The bus met everyone at the school house at seven-0-clock in the morning, it cost twenty five cents to ride the bus and twenty five cents to get into the fairgrounds. Doyle's neighbor was the driver of the bus and he did not have to pay the twenty five cents to ride. I set with Doyle on the bus and I found out that in his pocket, he only had a total of twenty five cents. He brought food in a paper bag to last the day, he would come to the bus to eat, no rides or games, and he could only see what was free. On the trip back home the bus stopped at a service station and I went in and bought two cokes, then they were five cents each, Doyle had a chicken sandwich left, so we split it and drank the cokes.

I remember exactly what happened because that morning I had an argument with my mother because she only gave me Fifteen dollars to spend at the fair that day, and I did not think that was enough. Then I find out Doyle had only twenty five cents.

Doyle was like this all the way thru school, broke, and never had any money. The state paid for his lunches in school and school supplies, and if he went to college they would help with that, because when he was in the third grade, he got an eye put out with a spitball, there in school, and he had one glass eye, so the school insurance helped him thru school.

Doyle finished the senior year with the highest average of anyone in the class; he would accept no honors or no help from anyone. He let it be known that he would not be at graduation. A few people knew why, it was because he did not have a suit, or shoes or anything he needed to go to a graduation.

The day before school was out, Doyle left and moved to Atlanta. A neighbor of theirs, that had a summer home here but lived in Atlanta, gave him a place to live in exchange for yard work, and it was only a fifteen minute walk to Ga. Tech. Doyle enrolled in a barber school to learn how to cut hair, in six months he had finished that school and had a job in a barbershop near Tech campus. He enrolled at Ga. Tech in the daytime and he cut hair at night. Then I lost track of Doyle.

I had found a good job in Texas and moved there, I was married and we had two sons, for years I wondered what ever happened to Doyle, but I never heard anything from him, and every one I ask said they had not heard anything. One year when I was back home I went to his uncles house to find out where Doyle was, and found out from a neighbor that both the uncle and aunt had passed away.

Twenty five years later I was back home for a visit, I had forgot all about Doyle, then I went to church on Sunday and someone taped me on the shoulder, when I turned around there was Doyle. He looked different, not the age, but his hair was combed, he had on expensive clothing and his shoes were nice and they were shined, his wife and four kids were dressed to the top, they had a son and three daughters.

We talked a long time, then we all went out to dinner and talked some more. Doyle had graduated from tech, he had gone on and got a doctorate degree, and now he was head engineer for the state of Ga. bridge division. Our two families spent the day together, just talking, we planned a fishing and hunting trip for the coming November, six months away.

Doyle's wife told me that day about the fishing trip that we had gone on many years ago, and about the trip to the fair in Atlanta, it seems that these two trips are the high points in his life, and he has never forgot about them, she said that he had told her about the trips several times.

In November we met at the Ramada Inn there in our hometown, he had his room and I had my room. On the first day there he called my room and ask if I could meet him in the restaurant right then, he said he had a problem he needed to discuss with me, so I said okay, I am on the way.

He told me that five days after we saw them in church on that Sunday, that he had won the lottery for twenty one million dollars. His wife did know it, but no one else in the family knows about it. He made me swear that I would tell no one other than my wife. There was an attorney in Charlestown S.C. that he went to college with, and he was a very close friend, he takes care of the money and keeps it invested. He pays the attorney ten thousand dollars a month to do this. There is a contract between the two of them that if the public finds out about the lottery money because of anything he did, he has to pay back all that he has received from Doyle's account.

I have my time in with the company I work for, and can retire anytime I want to, so when Doyle asks me to move back home and help him with his plan, I said that I would. Doyle had offered me whatever I wanted to move back, but we settled on the same salary that I was getting in Texas, and in sixty days, my family and I was back home and working for Doyle.

The lottery money was a gift from God, and it must be used to help people in need, and to work for the churches, any church, and no one will take credit for what is done, so it will be done in secret, this was Doyle's wish and his orders.

The only person, other than Doyle, that could write a check was the attorney, everything went thru him. He paid me on the first of the month. I hired who ever I wanted too, and the money was sent to me, so that I could pay them on the first day of the month. This system has been in effect for eleven years now, and Doyle has never written one check.

In the beginning I was given two orders on how and what to do. The first one was to stay in touch with the schools, and if any student in any school did not have lunch money or could not buy clothing or shoes to get in contact with that student and offer them a job. pay them well, no matter what kind of work they did. Doyle told me that people had offered him cloths and shoes, most of the time it was hand-me-downs and he would never accept them, he had too much pride, but no one ever offered him a way to make money, so he could work and pay for what he wanted.

The second order was to be involved with the churches, and to be sure their needs were met, the same rule on secrecy applied, no one was to know where it came from. This was the hard part. Doyle and I had agreed that we would attend different churches; He still lived in Atlanta but was home on weekends some of the time.

The first church that we went to had built a new church building three years ago, the building fund had a loan of one hundred and thirty thousand dollars, they were not behind and had never been behind, so now I am going to see how to pay this off without anyone knowing it. One of the deacons in the church was a loan officer in a bank that we did not do business with. I made an appointment with him and in his office we discussed this in secret. I told him it was not my money, but I told him nothing else. He agreed that if the money was honest money that he would work with us, and no one would ever know who paid what, and now it has been over ten years, he has paid over two million dollars to several different churches and he still works with us.

While Doyle was cutting hair and going to school at Ga. Tech, he had gone back to Cotton Tennessee to look for his sister Dot. He went to the grocery store to ask about her and found out that the family she lived with, had sold out and moved to Florida, but they did not know what town in Florida. Doyle wrote a letter and left it with the owners of the grocery store and he gave the phone number of the barbershop. It was nine years later when dot went to Cotton Tennessee to visit her foster family, they gave her the letter and she immediately called the number. The owner of the barbershop answered the phone, and told Dot that Doyle was not there but he would give him the message. Thirty minutes later Doyle called Dot and they had found each other. Dot was a school teacher in Florida.

There is as much money in the lottery account of Doyle's now, as there was when we started. The attorney, in S.C., has kept it invested and is just spending the interest. Doyle's son, an attorney also, and myself and the deacon loan officer are directors of the foundation, Doyle's will directs what is to be done with the money in this account, his family is well off, with his retirement and investments he had made.

Today is the first time that I met the attorney, and it is the first time that all four of us that work together, have been together at the same time, and we are here for Doyle's funeral.

What has been done so far is all good, what gets done in the future is up to the way the four of us decide to expand and cover more area.

We all know that we can cause things to happen, we can cause a school kid to find a job when they need it most, we can cause bills to be paid anonymously, there is a lot of good things that can be done with Doyle's lottery money.

This foundation owns no property. It leases two cars and has a lease on a building in town, one block from the school, the kids do all the work here, and they have to work to be paid, and everyone is paid the same amount per hour. If they are under thirteen years old we do pay for lunches, and we have paid for clothing and if the need is there we will do it again.

These kids do not ask for help. If it is obvious they are in need, they are offered a job. They do not know Doyle

Bradshaw, and have never heard of him, but because of Doyle they can get help when they need it, and because of this, Doyle is receiving his reward now.

End Of Story/Author & Narrator Larry English